THE DANCE

OF THE

NECKLACE

ooo

THE DANCE

OF THE

NECKLACE

by

GRAZIA DELEDDA

OOO

Translated with an Introduction by

Mary Ann Frese Witt
&
Martha Witt

ITALICA PRESS
NEW YORK & BRISTOL
2023

Italian Original
La danza della collana

Translation & Introduction Copyright © 2023
Mary Ann Frese Witt and Martha Witt

Italica Press Modern Italian Fiction Series

ITALICA PRESS, INC.
99 Wall Street, Suite 650
New York, New York 10005

Library of Congress Cataloging-in-Publication Data
Names: Deledda, Grazia, 1871-1936, author. | Witt, Martha, translator, writer of introduction. | Witt, Mary Ann Frese, translator, writer of introduction.
Title: The dance of the necklace / Grazia Deledda ; [translation & introduction, Mary Ann Frese Witt and Martha Witt].
Other titles: Danza della collana. English
Description: New York : Italica Press, 2023. | Series: Italica press modern Italian fiction series | Includes bibliographical references. | Summary: "Originally published in Italian in 1924, this novel by Nobel-Prize winner Grazia Deledda tells the stoy of a valuable string of pearls that comes to symbolize the dance of passions: jealousy and greed, and erotic and familial love which unite and divide the three main characters"-- Provided by publisher.
Identifiers: LCCN 2022061573 (print) | LCCN 2022061574 (ebook) | ISBN 9781599104485 (hardcover) | ISBN 9781599104492 (trade paperback) | ISBN 9781599104508 (kindle edition) | ISBN 9781599104515 (pdf)
Subjects: LCGFT: Novels.
Classification: LCC PQ4811.E6 D3613 2023 (print) | LCC PQ4811.E6 (ebook) | DDC 853/.912--dc23/eng/20230117
LC record available at https://lccn.loc.gov/2022061573
LC ebook record available at https://lccn.loc.gov/2022061574

Cover Photo: Evelyn Nesbit Thaw (1920) by Orval Hixon, Museum of Photographic Arts, San Diego CA. https://commons.wikimedia.org/wiki/File:Evelyn_Nesbit_Thaw,_1920_(5711528268).jpg

For a Complete List of Titles in Italian Literature
Visit our Web Site at:
www.ItalicaPress.com

About the Translators

Mary Ann Frese Witt is Professor Emerita of Italian, French, and Comparative Literature at North Carolina State University. Her books include *The Search for Modern Tragedy: Aesthetic Fascism in Italy and France* (Cornell University Press, 2001) and *Metatheater and Modernity: Baroque and Neobaroque* (Fairleigh Dickinson University Press, 2013). She has published numerous articles on Pirandello and modern theater. In collaboration with Martha King, she is the translator of Pirandello's novel *Her Husband* (Duke University Press, 2000). In collaboration with Martha Witt, she has translated and published contemporary Italian short stories, two plays by Pirandello — *Six Characters in Search of an Author* (Italica Press, 2013) and *Henry IV* (Italica Press, 2016) — and Grazia Deledda's novel *Ivy (L'Edera)* (Italica Press, 2019).

Martha Witt is Professor of English and Creative Writing at William Paterson University. She is the author of the novel, *Broken As Things Are* (Holt, 2004/Picador, 2005). Her translations and short fiction have appeared in multiple anthologies and international literary journals. In collaboration with Mary Ann Frese Witt, she has translated and published contemporary Italian short stories, two plays by Pirandello — *Six Characters in Search of an Author* (Italica Press, 2013) and *Henry IV* (Italica Press, 2016) — and Grazia Deledda's novel *Ivy* (Italica Press, 2019).

INTRODUCTION

Grazia Maria Cosima Damiana Deledda (1871–1936) spent the first thirty years of her life in the town of Nuoro on the island of Sardinia. Although her native language was a Sardinian dialect, she wrote entirely in Italian. By the late nineteenth century, women writers had become well-known and popular in England, the United States, France, and even Italy, but the idea of a woman writing in Sardinia was shocking. As a teenager with only an elementary-school education, Deledda began to write stories based on her family and her native island. Although she spent the major part of her career in Rome, much of her creative work continued to be rooted in the landscape, characters, and customs of Sardinia. Deledda, who referred to her hometown of Nuoro as a "bronze-age village," knew that, in order to further her writing career, she would need to leave Sardinia for Rome or Milan. She also knew that she could never make such a move as a single woman. At the age of twenty-eight, already considered an "old maid," Deledda married Palmiro Madesani, and the couple moved to Rome. Once settled in that city, Madesani became, effectively, his wife's business manager and promoter. (He was heavily satirized by Luigi Pirandello in his novel *Suo marito*.[1]) In Rome, Deledda maintained a schedule devoted to domestic duties in the mornings and writing in the afternoons.

Despite her move to the metropolis, Deledda's homeland continued to fuel her imagination. Her writing reflects both her literary apprenticeship in an agrarian–pastoral civilization with primeval roots, shaped by myths, and archetypes, as well as her experience in an urban, literary society. Imbued by this particular combination, Deledda's fictional worlds continued to resonate

1. Published in Italian in 1911 and in English in 2000 as *Her Husband*, translated by Martha King and Mary Ann Frese Witt (Duke University Press).

deeply with readers across Europe, and Deledda quickly became an acclaimed writer in literary as well as popular circles.

Deledda's first major success was the novel *Elias Portolu*,[2] published in 1900 in installments in the prestigious literary journal *La Nuova Antologia*. Critics discerned the influence of Dostoevsky in the novel. Deledda was indeed an avid reader of Russian literature, once commenting that "the primitive life" of Russian people bore a similarity to life in Sardinia. *Elias Portolu* was almost immediately translated into French by Georges Herelle for *La Revue des deux mondes*.

By 1904, Deledda had two children and declared her first interest to be maternity. As a mother, however, she continued to write and publish. Significant novels include *Dopo il divorzio* (1902), *Cenere* (1904), *L'Edera* (1908), *Canne al vento* (1913), *Marianna Sirca* (1915), *La Madre* (1920), *La danza della collana* (1924), and *Cosima* (published posthumously in 1937). Deledda's short stories, which combine fantasy elements and often feature popular legends, superstitions, and magical powers, also drew critical attention. Deledda received the Nobel Prize for Literature in 1926, the second woman to receive this award and the only Italian woman to have done so.

Although Deledda remained on the Italian continent, she never cut ties with her native Sardinia. During her girlhood in Nuoro, friends and neighbors had resented her early journal publications. But as an acclaimed writer, Deledda served to counteract the ruling stereotype of Sardinians as backward, uneducated, and uncouth. The islanders took pride in their native daughter and her talent, which had revealed to the world those truths about Sardinia and the Sardinian character that only fiction can fully render. After her death of heart failure due to breast cancer in 1936, Deledda

---

2. Translated by Martha King (Northwestern University Press 1995).

was buried in Cervia, near Rome, sparking controversy among the Sardinians, who wanted her buried back "home." It was not until 1959, after some disputes about the orthodoxy of her religion, that her body was transported to Sardinia where it was buried in a cemetery near Nuoro. The Deledda family house is now the Museo Deleddiano, and the island people preserve her memory. Her work, which has found its place in the canon of Italian literature, continues to serve as a guide to the island's rich and often misunderstood history and culture.

In Italy, Deledda's novels were initially classified as belonging entirely to *verismo*, the Italian version of realism or naturalism associated with the Sicilian Giovanni Verga (1840–1922). Anglophone readers of Deledda's novels, many of which remain untranslated into English, have been influenced by D.H. Lawrence, whose interest in Sardinia dated from his *Sea and Sardinia* (1921) and who wrote a preface to *The Woman and the Priest*, published in 1923, a reprint of Mary Steegman's translation of *La Madre*, originally published in Britain as *The Mother* in 1922. Although Lawrence rates Deledda as a novelist superior to her contemporaries Gabriele D'Annunzio and Matilde Serao, he declares in the preface that she is "not a first-class genius." Lawrence goes on to state that "what she does do is to create the passionate complex of a primitive populace." In line with his own interests, Lawrence is of the opinion that the "primitive," isolated society depicted by Deledda is governed by "the rigid conventions of barbarism, and at the same time, the fierce violence of the instinctive passions." Deledda portrays instinctive sexuality frustrated by barbaric (along with Catholic) conventions. Comically, Lawrence extends the notion of "instinctive" to the Italian language when discussing the difficulties of translating Deledda into English. "In the mouths of the simple people, Italian is a purely instinctive language…almost impossible to reproduce in the more cut-and-dried northern languages." Although Lawrence's remarks on the conflict between instinctual passion and societal rules in Deledda's work are to some extent valuable, his portrayal of Sardinia as barbaric and isolated reproduces the ruling stereotype of the time and neglects the island's complex 4,000-year-old history. He reinforced a view of Deledda's work that prevailed for some time, seeing her as a purely Sardinian writer, uninterested in plot, character, and a more universal exploration of themes and emotions. Recently, critics have explored feminism, symbolism, and even modernism in Deledda's novels. Deledda read Balzac, Zola, and Manzoni, but she also read Dostoevsky, Schopenhauer, and Nietzsche.

Though Deledda has, in the past, been discounted as a regional writer, renewed critical interest in her work has identified a deep affinity with European modernism. In *Grazia Deledda's Dance of Modernity*, Margherita Heyer-Caput argues that Deledda relates to modernism "not in spite of but because of her Sardinian vantage point."[3] Unlike Deledda's earlier work, *The Dance of the Necklace* is not primarily concerned with Sardinia. Instead of being set in the Sardinian countryside, the narrative unfolds in an unspecified city. In a 1923 letter to her friend Marino Moretti, she writes of the novel: "I have finished a story that, according to my intentions, takes place in a big city and demonstrates the vain anguish of our strongest passions: love, ambition, and the instinct to appear more than what we are."[4] The city, however, is not prominently featured in the story. The house where the two principal female characters live, aunt and niece, both named Maria Baldi, is isolated. Giovanni Delys, the young count who enters their lives, does go into the city with the younger Maria, but most of that scene's action takes place in a church, where the two fall in love. The "necklace" referred to in the title is a valuable string of pearls

3.   Margherita Heyer-Caput, *Grazia Deledda's Dance of Modernity* (Toronto: Toronto University Press, 2008), 11.
4.   Heyer-Caput, 188.

that Giovanni's family had given the elder Maria Baldi as collateral for a debt. It comes to symbolize the "dance" of passions: amorous and familial love, jealousy, and greed that both unite and divide the three characters. One of the most fascinating aspects of this novel is the particular relationship that develops between Delys and the older Maria Baldi, who, in Deledda's inimitable style, reflects on what it means to be a woman, alone and aging, yet still full of feelings and desires in a world where she is becoming increasingly unwanted and invisible. Deledda's concentration on her characters' relations and emotions brings this work closer to the modernism of its time as opposed to the naturalism of her previous novels.

As translators of Deledda's work, we remain conscious of the fact that literary translation is often viewed as either too easy or too difficult. The believers in "too easy" argue that translation is a matter of substituting one word for another, greatly facilitated by digital programs such as Google Translate. The advocates of "too difficult" argue that the creative originality of a writer in his or her original language can never be adequately represented in another language, no matter how skilled the translator. The former is easier to refute than the latter. A dictionary, printed or electronic, will often give several equivalents in English to a word in Italian and sometimes none of them fit the context in the original. Translation software can be useful: it can also be laughably off base.

On the other hand, there is some truth in the opinion that literary translation is too difficult, or even impossible. No translation is ever definitive: Homer has been re-translated many times before and after Chapman. Numerous poets, scholars, and other skilled translators continue to translate Dante's *Commedia*. If we continue to translate, just as we continue to write, it is with the knowledge that translation relies, at some level, on the translator's interpretation of the original as well as the ever-evolving socio-cultural context in which that translated work is published; therefore, there is no definitive translation. Most translators would maintain that there is no such thing as a literal translation. Joseph Farell, who translated Dario Fo, argues that the ideal translation combines "fidelity and flair." Italo Calvino, who translated several novels from French while writing his own, stated that "translating is the true way of reading a text. One reads only when one translates" (our translation).

It is important to keep in mind that Grazia Deledda was, herself, a translator. Not only had she translated Balzac's *Eugénie Grandet* into Italian (1930), but her own works are, in a sense, translations from her mother tongue, Sardo. The literal meaning of translation, from the Latin *translatio,* is to "carry over," and one of the joys in translating Deledda is the sense of navigating the two languages of the original text while trying to "carry over" the foreign culture to the familiar one. Translating Deledda involves a particular attention to word choice, nuances, musicality, and allusions, considerations that inevitably lead to a deeper appreciation of her work.

Of course, writing in Italian rather than her native dialect, facilitated Deledda's early national success. Considering, however, her range, scope, and eventual fame as a writer beyond her national borders, particularly in France and Spain, Deledda's relative obscurity in the English-speaking world is startling. Fortunately, recent translations and scholarship have reignited an interest in Deledda's work, which resonates more than a century later, in ways that Deledda herself could not have anticipated. With the publication of *The Dance of the Necklace*, we seek to lend our own efforts in broadening the readership of this important, historically and culturally relevant woman writer. Readers, scholars, and translators fortunate enough to have spent time with Grazia

Deledda's work will agree that she deserves the enthusiastic following in English that her male contemporaries Giovanni Verga and Luigi Pirandello have enjoyed.

ooo

Deledda's Novels in Translation:
A Chronological List

Nostalgia, translated by Helen Hester Colvill, Chapman and Hall, 1905.

After the Divorce, translated by Maria Hornor Landsdale (aka Katherine Wyldeand) in 1905 and then by Susan Ashe, Northwestern Press, 1995.

Ashes, translated by Maria Hornor Landsdale (aka Katherine Wyldeand), 1908 and then by Jan Kozma, Fairleigh Dickinson University Press, 2004.

The Mother and the Priest, translated by Mary Steegman and originally published in 1922, reprinted with a forward by D.H. Lawrence, Macmillan, 1923.

Cosima, translated by Martha King, Italica Press, 1988.

Elias Portolu, translated by Martha King, Northwestern University Press, 1995.

The Church of Solitude, translated by E. Ann Matter, SUNY Press, 2002.

Reeds in the Wind, translated by Martha King, Italica Press, 2008.

Ivy, translated by Martha Witt and Mary Ann Frese Witt, Italica Press, 2019.

The Flight into Egypt, translated by Kevan Houser, ISBN Services, 2020.

Chiaroscuro translated by Kevan Houser, ISBN Services, 2021.

The Dance of the Necklace, translated by Martha Witt and Mary Ann Frese Witt, Italica Press, 2023.

THE DANCE

OF THE

NECKLACE

ooo

The winter bark cracks. Red veins among the black clouds and green shades on the dark earth proclaim the return of spring. Toward sunset, the new moon appears in the bright west like a boat that, after a successful journey, happily returns to port. Its bluish glow reflects off the dark green of the laurels down in the remains of gardens invaded by a sea of new buildings.

Against the background of this horizon, the new city takes shape with its white buildings, their aerial terraces festooned by clothes hung out to dry. A few dark cypresses are brightened by the liquid color of the sky surrounding them. Down from this mountain of buildings, which infuses the damp air with the scent of lime and whitewash, flow rivers of still-unfinished roads, rivers of flint between granite sidewalks that furrow the still-bare meadows and lose themselves among the reeds and junipers of the countryside.

A man, who had also come down from the city along these streets, stopped right at the edge of a meadow where the houses of a new neighborhood end. He looked at the last of the small houses, a little detached from the others, which, however, did not appear to have been recently built.

There stands a two-story house with no garden, only a large piece of land enclosed by an iron fence. The green shutters are closed against the grainy gray façade. Also closed is the little door varnished to a sheen, hidden away at the top of two marble steps, its large brass studs and oval plaque bearing the owner's name and shining like gold.

Only the window on the upper floor is open, and the white curtain that occasionally flutters seems to want to encourage the man to cross the gap created by the river of road.

He crosses but hesitates before climbing the steps toward the door, almost as if preparing to climb a mountain. His eyes are sharp enough to read the name engraved on the brass plate, "Maria Baldi," and since it is precisely this Maria Baldi he seeks, he plucks up his courage for the climb and stretches out a finger to press the doorbell.

Then he hesitates again and looks at the door as though looking at a stranger's face. The brass keyholes seem to be two unfamiliar eyes. They stare back at him, grotesquely reflecting his own face so that it resembles the face of a drunken mulatto.

It is a ridiculous face that, nevertheless, frightens him. But he reacts. A mysterious challenge immediately rises up between him and the goblins inside that guard the closed house. You will not ring. You cannot ring, and you know why.

He touched the cold doorbell but could not press it. He felt as though an inner thread were pulling back his hand, but he heard a step inside the house, a step approaching the door, as though someone inside had peeped out and was coming to open it, and he rang.

When the door opened wide, he felt blood rush to his face with an almost wild charge of joy, so much so that the woman who had opened the door was infused by its reflection. And they both seemed to shudder, like two people who had once known each other well and had not seen each other for a long time.

The woman was dressed to go out. Her reddish cloak with gold embroidery on the flaps resembled folded wings, and the little black velvet cap with two feather pins made her look like a butterfly.

"Are you Signorina Baldi?" the man asked in a clear voice.

She gave a slight nod, accompanied by a timid and bashful flutter of her eyelashes. Reassured, he said, "I don't want to inconvenience you, because I see you're on your way out. It's about your land next door, for a possible sale."

This news frightened her more, discomposing her fine dark face, lit by bright greenish eyes which, dimmed by the shadow of her long eyelashes and knit eyebrows, resembled two lakes in the middle of the woods.

"Who told you that the land is for sale?" she asked, as though responding to an insult.

He answered in the same tone, as though to justify himself, "An agency, Signorina. I have your address here, and a map of the neighborhood. But I have also been informed that you have no intention of selling for the time being. And you are right. Prices are rising every day. However, the offer would be very advantageous. Is it really not possible to negotiate?"

"I'm sorry, no. At least not for now."

However, she seemed a little uncertain, so he insisted, "You will at least allow me to leave you my address and ask you to remember me in case you decide to sell."

She hesitatingly took the card he handed her, as though only out of politeness. She looked at it and raised her eyes, reassured. Shielded and illuminated by a small crown, appeared a beautiful name:

Count Giovanni Delys

A count is always, in a woman's eyes, something more than a common man, and the one who bore this title appeared to deserve it, with his tall, straight figure, and elegant clothes. Above all, it was the way he deigned to look at the owner of the land with great interest and in a manner that made her feel she wasn't simply being flattered, especially since she knew the land's very high value. But that thought darkened her eyes again and pushed her out the door, which she pulled behind her.

The man felt rejected but remained firm, standing his ground.

"The transfer of the land…again, please excuse the question, is solely up to you?"

"Not up to me alone. That is," she answered, suddenly confident and almost tough. "Yes, it's up to me, if I choose. I haven't decided yet because I'm intending to build on it myself."

This news almost seemed to cheer the man. His lively black eyes, which did not stop staring at the woman, turned toward the ground.

"The location is magnificent, and if you have the means, it's a pity not to build there right away. But it's even more of a pity that I can't build there myself," he added, smiling.

He had a mocking, melancholy smile, which suddenly rejuvenated his long, sunken, clean-shaven face, but allowed his healthy teeth, a few already gold-capped, to show too much.

This smile also pleased the woman. That large mouth, mean and sad, aroused a desire in her, and suddenly she seemed quite interested in his affairs. She went down a step and with her bare hand, pointed toward a space still free of buildings.

"You see, everything there is still for sale, and for a good price. The land is owned by a cooperative that will even take charge of the construction."

He followed her hand with a gaze as tenacious as a kiss.

"I know, I know, but it was your land I wanted."

She made a vague gesture as though to say, "If it were only up to me, I'd satisfy your wish." She then went back up the step and turned to close the door.

He didn't leave. When she turned to wave goodbye, she saw that his face looked so hollow and saddened that she almost felt pity. It seemed to her that he wanted to ask her something else, perhaps to accompany him, not to leave him by himself on the edge of the mysterious city which, on that lonely day — it was a Saturday and the workers were not working — looked made of ruins.

But he quickly pulled himself together, waved good-bye, and let her go.

She walked away with a silent, agile step, sure of herself on the very high heels of those shiny shoes that reflected the golden color of her sheer stockings. The hard flesh of her slender legs seemed to shine through that veil. Her coat and short dress fluttered together, lightly, moving with pleasure and jokingly, happy to be spinning about. And her entire harmonious figure, against the backdrop of those long new roads that did not end, even at the horizon, seemed made for her, leading her into the world as she moved with a dance step on the arch between the heel and toe of those bright little shoes.

The man followed her, keeping his distance and without meaning to, also walked lightly, almost trying not to make noise so that she would not notice. But he understood that she was well aware of this pursuit, and was satisfied with it, and that, if he wished, she would no longer go where she had intended to go before she met him, but to a place where they could meet again. The landowner and the man speculating on the land had disappeared, and in their place remained only the woman walking through the paths of the world, content with herself and her beauty, and the male pursuing her.

The road widened, opening onto a piazza, which it seemed to escape on all sides into other streets happily filled with villas and gardens against backdrops of blue and silver. It continued upwards, engulfed by large buildings, and yet still deserted, still belonging only to the man and the woman. In the background, though, one could see the flow and crisscrossing of vehicles, the movement of a crowd, and hear the screech and roar of the living city.

The woman quickened her pace as though someone down there were calling to her and waiting for her. The man, too, hurried on, driven by a sense of jealousy, or by the instinct of the hunter who sees his prey losing itself and saving itself in the bush. She turned at the top of the road, still following the sidewalk on the left, and he arrived in time to meet her gaze. It seemed to him that, in the midst of the gray crowd, the color of her coat spread like a warm burst of sunlight that reached him. Because of her quick gait, she looked as though she were skating, circling around the people in her way, forging her own path.

He saw her hesitate only a moment before a large door, almost as though she had to enter, either because she was headed there, or to escape the man pursuing her. He then instinctively began to run, but she was already through the door, faster still, as if she had felt his imperceptible anxiety and was further enticing him to try to reach her.

She turns again, and then disappears again at the corner of another street. Now it is indeed time to run, and the man reclaims his youthful agility in order to finally catch up to her.

And he is not surprised to see her pushing open a carved door, guarded by a sort of blind hermit whose hand, hollow and wooden as a ladle, is stretched out begging.

It is a church door.

The church was illuminated by the glow of a pyramid of fake candles with electric light rising like the pipes of an organ above the high altar. To the man, the altar seemed to ascend into an indefinite distance, behind a high iron gate enclosing it like an enchanted garden against a backdrop of gilding and mosaics and stained-glass windows that, unlike the candles, shone almost furtively.

He stood at the end of the dark nave, his hat and cane hidden by his side. As he gradually grew accustomed to the half-light, he began to distinguish, among the flock of women filling the church with their breath and perfumes, her figure bent over a kneeler, her wings spread to the ground like an angel's before God.

"Is she praying, or is she thinking of me?"

He felt sure that she was both praying and thinking of him. They stood immobile as insects sucking at the same flower before rising and meeting each other in the light. And suddenly the church seemed to come to light just for them. For them, a young priest dressed in gold went up to the altar and prayed, then he climbed up to the radiant pulpit and seemed to address only them, speaking of the vanity of things and how men in search of the pleasures of the flesh had lost their way.

His voice was mechanical and declamatory, but when he spoke about God's invocation to the soul, to call it to His love as the lover calls to the woman he loves,

"Come, my beloved,…"

his voice grew warm with a virile sensuality. Perhaps he himself was calling a beloved woman to his hidden passion, and all was aflame in the golden vessel of the pulpit. And the faces of the women paled as if each of them was the one being summoned. Even the man below, leaning against the cold wall, felt a rush of heat down his back as though the entire church were suddenly on fire.

On tiptoe he went to sit in an empty front pew and looked again at the woman, feeling revitalized. He felt that some inner force already united them, as the word of God came down upon them from a soul in the throes of passion, and that she, too, must be trembling at the call of eternal love.

The entire ceremony took on a nuptial hue when the organ and the choral chanting of nuns filled the atmosphere with the murmur and trembling of trees in a forest in the moonlight.

The walls open, and they are surrounded by the vastness of infinity. Sound and song descend from above, from a hidden height that at times seems very far away, and at other times seems to swell just over the heads of the faithful.

The man closes his eyes as though overcome by sleep. He feels he has emerged from the forest and has detached himself from the earth. And he travels by sea, like a sick Tristan, toward an undiscovered country where his life should begin again and renew itself from the roots.

It is night. Only the twinkling of the stars lights the vast infinity of water and sky, and the sea sings with that organ voice, austere and powerful, like the voice of God.

He watches his past detach and move away from him like the outline of the land he left behind: the large villa by the sea where he was born, the fishermen's village, and the dark little town engraved like an etching on the sandy yellow plain with a few greenish spots and a few streaks of ochre against the backdrop of pale sky. The beach that absorbed all the joy of his childhood, the dreams of his adolescence, and the murky pains of youth, suddenly darkens like a spring day overcast by a storm. Everything appeared to him the same as it had been, but in a different light, never before seen, like a landscape viewed from the sea that seems to recede from itself and dissolve as though made of clouds.

Then, from the grandiose sounds of the organ and the choir, surged a voice like pure mountain water. It was a woman's voice. Little by little it rose above all the other sounds and seemed to become light. The words of the sacred chant crumbled into it like diamonds into dust, and it was no longer a chant but a series of cries, sometimes imploring, sometimes menacing, always passionate and filled with a moan of desire. Like the sound of the organ pipes, these other sounds rose from a single depth, where the great human passions shook, struggling against each other, the heaving of flesh and spirit towards an unattainable good.

And the man standing below, lulled by that movement of the waves that carried him outside time and space, recalled the story of a woman — young, beautiful, and very rich — who had become a nun for love and sang to exhale her pain. Her cry crossed the walls of the convent, rose to the sky, and fell on the world with the tears of the stars, no longer the lament of a woman bound by her passion, but the universal song of the imprisoned spirit of the earth.

When the chorus died down, and he thought that his ship had anchored, he opened his eyes again and felt them moist with tears. This irritated him. A man must not cry, even when facing the greatest misery. He got up abruptly, went back to the wall beside the door, and waited for her to come out.

People were leaving, slowly, one after the other, in a line, exactly like passengers disembarking when their ship arrives.

She was among the last. Her eyes, as though gilded by candlelight, met the man's. In a single moment, the vital pact was concluded. From the morning of the next day onward, the woman began to wait.

He did not reappear, not in the church, nor elsewhere, but she felt that he must come back. That the glance caught in the half-light of the church had already sealed their fate. Deep down, she was afraid of deluding herself, for she knew that the life she was forced to live led her towards dreaming. She lived in that large house, still as isolated as a villa in the country, with an elderly relative who watched over her, and since she had been the one to raise her, controlled her every action.

In the morning, the merchants brought everything to the house, then the two women did their housework together, assisted in the dirtiest jobs by an old servant, deaf as a stone. In the afternoon, the young woman went out almost every day, and at night, she read until late. She read novels and the society pages of the newspapers as well as accounts of famous trials and extraordinary events.

These readings, done almost in secret, in the mystery of night, worked in her mind like unhealthy food in the body. They nourished her with murky dreams that spread a veil of fog over the reality of life.

Finally, one day, she saw a coach stopping in front of the door. A man got out and put a letter in the mailbox, then he drove off again. She rushed down the stairs, as she did as a child, barely touching the banister. She took the letter and hid it in her bosom.

Why was she hiding it? She didn't really know. She only felt her heart beating against the letter, which in a mysterious conversation, answered as though it had a heart of its own.

The man was only asking that she receive him or make an appointment, nothing else, and he sent a respectful salutation, yet she looked at the little piece of paper with giddiness.

The handwriting was so neatly etched that it resembled print: even the address on the envelope, stiff and black, left her almost anguished, and she felt as if she was reading his name for the first time.

The paper and the envelope were square, rather small, sturdy: everything about the man denoted a sense of order, toughness, even calculation. Perhaps, though, that was only the deliberate masking of a passionate and disordered nature aware of itself and wanting to exert control.

Even the delay in seeing and hearing from him demonstrated a resolute seriousness. Perhaps he had struggled against his feelings, barely allowing himself to win, giving in at last to his passion as he felt it ripen, the way fruit falls from a tree. And the woman, who instinctively knew these things, thought she need only bend over and pluck the fruit.

She answered by making an appointment in a public garden.

When she arrived on time and seemingly calm, wearing a cloak too heavy for the early warmth of that late winter afternoon, she saw the man waiting for her. Dressed in gray, stylish and refined down to the smallest details, he appeared younger than when she last saw him, despite the wrinkle of austerity in his face, which expected but did not smile at her arrival.

Maybe he's suspicious because I didn't receive him at home, she thought at once. And she had an excuse ready.

"Please forgive me for meeting you here. I have a house full of relatives who have come for the holidays. Among others, there is a sick aunt."

He let a moment pass in silence, allowing the useless lie to fall and vanish. In the meantime, they sat down on a bench in an isolated spot by the pond.

"Signorina," he asked softly, looking far into the distance, "do you know why I want to speak to you?"

And she, who realized he had not been deceived by her initial words, attempted to make amends with an outburst of sincerity. "I know."

Then he turned to look at her. The golden shadow of the elm-trees bronzed the pallor of her downturned face, and it seemed as if she had purposely chosen a place that created the illusion of a shelter in the woods high above the lake's shore as the only suitable background for her image.

"Look at me," he begged.

And their eyes meet again, mirrored in infinity, but the blue-green reflection in the water, moved by a slight dark quivering, seems to prevent them once more from fully revealing themselves.

He turns again in profile, leans back on the bench, crosses his nimble legs, and pulls his trousers up to his knees, revealing gray silk stockings. He begins to speak in a calm, cold voice that gradually, only when he forgets to control it, takes on a warm tone, like a pale face blushing. "Now, I'll tell you about myself. You know my name and also my title, which I can sincerely tell you I care about as one cares about one's own appearance and character. I am an aristocrat by nature, and that means that I like things that are beautiful and refined and being surrounded by order, silence, cleanliness, and space. My room might be bare, but it must be large and have a painting or a small work of art along with my lamp to keep my soul company. And I don't mind not partaking in the so-called "brilliant" life, pleasant as it is with luxury, movement, and color, as long as my days and evenings pass without boredom, without encountering vulgarity, without having to reproach myself for anything humiliating or self-diminishing. After all, I am a loner, perhaps a dreamer, perhaps even a mystic."

Grazia Deledda

After a slight pause he resumed. "And I must now tell you that I am not rich, as you may think. Don't make that gesture of protest. Wealth is one of the greatest strengths a man can possess if he knows how to use it because he understands its true and intimate value. I, unfortunately, am not rich. I do, however, have something saved from the wreckage of what was once true family wealth. My father, who really did not know its value, or perhaps because he was the last of a race exhausted by pleasure and by possessing everything, sought in life only gratification, uncommon emotions, risk, and adventure. He had surrounded himself with a court of friends, parasites, useless servants. He traveled and gambled. The unfortunate man even tried to speculate on things he knew nothing about and thus gambled away his entire fortune. My mother was not aware of his ruin until his final years when a long and sad illness — perhaps the consequence of his sprees — sent him back home and forced him into a slow atonement. My mother was religious, too religious. This was her only weakness. She accepted everything as God's will and did not know how to oppose the force of evil that sucked out our lives and our wealth. In any case, according to her, everything was saved because our name was saved. Even her dowry was sold, and the other properties included a fourteenth-century castle, still intact with its perfectly preserved three towers, the keep, and the entire interior. The furniture, the weapons, the works of art, and even the locks are from that period. I spent my early childhood there. On one side, the castle looks out over a large, lonely, uncultivated valley; on the other, it overlooks the short plateau where the small village is located, below which the valley descends, completely deserted for kilometers. In winter, wolves approach the village, but the inhabitants are brave and even the women know how to handle a rifle. When my father died, the castle was sold, partly because the upkeep and the staff cost an incredible amount of money. But the years spent in that grandiose solitude, in that silent but authentic splendor, in the company of those portraits of gentlemen and beautiful women who were more than alive to me, have certainly molded my soul, and perhaps my body as well, into an immutable form.

"Even now, at night, when I awaken, I feel like I am there, listening to the whirling of the wind around the towers that appropriates the howling of the wolf or the infinite silence of spring nights.

"In the summertime, we went down to our villa by the sea, where, in fact, I was born. We later ended up taking refuge there for good. My mother closed herself up as though in a convent. She died there, assisted by my nurse who is still there, guarding our memories.

"This villa, too, is old and large, and the revenue from it, especially in the summer months, is my main source of income. I spent my adolescence there, intertwined with happiness and sorrow, with anxiety and dreams about the future. Afterwards, my life faded away: I studied law, I became a soldier. My mother died last year, happy to have fulfilled her duty towards me, leaving me to face life armed with experience and awareness, without great illusions and yet also with a residue of faith: a real man, that is. Chance has brought me to you, chance which is, after all, the chain of this necklace of days that make up life. To tell you the truth, my mother's death left me a bit stunned. She was my only support, even from afar. She was the holy image of my faith in life, the soul of the house. And I grew up too afraid of the world that had devoured my father. I lived too long in the house to be able to detach myself from it. I'll tell you something that seems romantic but isn't. As soon as you appeared, I felt as though I were having a sunstroke, not so much because of your extraordinary beauty as because of your resemblance to a portrait of an unknown woman. Her portrait hung in a connecting room in the castle, and she seemed to be looking at me every time I happened to stand beneath her blue-green eyes, as though she were waiting for me to speak in order to come alive and answer me. I was afraid of her and hurried past.

"Perhaps I am superstitious. I believe in a fantasy world where our ego, split in two, lives out its best half, which is that of the soul. I am still the child who fearfully crosses the hall of the lonely castle instead of trying to find the right word to begin a conversation with that unknown woman, who, after all, represents life. But you will perform the miracle: you will speak to me now. Perhaps you will be the one to say the first real word in this great conversation."

She was shaking all over. She felt that, had he brushed her with his finger, she would have fallen to the ground, melting into tears of blood like the split pomegranate that falls from the tree when the wind blows. Her face, especially her eyes, reflected the indefinable flickering of the lake, as if they too were made of water and light.

"What can I tell you?" she murmured, wringing her hands a little, desperate yet exalted. "If, for you, I am really, at this moment, the personification of life, it is a very poor life that you choose for yourself. But perhaps I will become enriched because of you and become, as I hope, the manifestation of your dream. Chance, which, as you rightly say, constitutes the chain of the necklace of our days, could not have pushed us so far in vain. You too perhaps know something about me. I am humble and small before you, so different and yet so similar to you! I am a daughter of the people, but I also care about my origins, because from the true people, those closest to the earth, I derive my strength and my desire to live. Perhaps in this way I truly represent life, like the things that spring from the earth, sown by God. Like all my relatives, I came here to the big city from an isolated town — a town in the mountains where the inhabitants, after being shepherds for centuries, suddenly became builders. We came down here to build the town: my father, my brothers, my cousins, my uncles, all of them bricklayers, pavers, stonemasons, all of them good at their jobs, perhaps because of their old habits and their familiarity with stones and volcanic rock. Some of them became master builders, contractors, then, finally, owners of their buildings, and they grew rich. When I was a little girl, I, too, worked in the factories where my relatives climbed up and worked. Too often, unfortunately, a few fell down, buckets of lime and bricks in their hands, crashing to their deaths, as though against the cliffs of their native mountains. Then times changed. We ourselves became owners. I went to school, not for long, but I did go to school. I have read, and I read a lot, and my mind has opened up. My intelligence has developed. I live alone with a relative who doesn't love me and only stays with me because I am useful to her. Little by little our family has dispersed. My parents are dead, and the other relatives have gone back to their town and live their own lives. After all, I too am a loner, a dreamer. But I also know how to look life in the face and work and be self-sufficient. So far, I haven't met anyone able to love me and know me and especially to get me to love him. Men turn to look at me, yes, and follow me, but only for how I appear on the outside, whereas I would like to be loved for myself, for how I might be valued on the inside, because I also firmly believe in a higher life where only the soul exists."

Without looking at her, he said, "I'm happy to hear you speak this way. The fact that you have chosen this dreamlike spot in the garden for our first meeting proves your instinct for finesse and sophistication. We have crossed the busy, dusty city to arrive here, so, I hope, we will happily cross the difficulties and ugliness of life to meet at a point that will be the last and best stop on our earthly journey."

"Yes, yes," she said impetuously.

"How do you live?" he asked softly. There was already a sense of closeness in his subdued manner of speaking. And she answered softly, as well, as though to avoid being heard by someone listening in.

"I live a seemingly quiet, industrious, and secure life. Sad and empty, really. My days are always the same. I get up early as a matter of habit, and I work with my relative and a woman who comes to do the hardest chores. The house is big, and I like to keep it clean. The bottom floor is rented to a family that is gone almost all year round, so it is very quiet but also requires a lot of vigilance. My relative never goes out for fear of thieves. I, on the other hand, go out in the afternoon almost every day. I have few acquaintances and no friends. I like to go out alone, to walk, to rest in the gardens, to look in shop windows, to get lost in the crowd, carried away by it. I often go to church, partly out of devotion, partly because I like hymns, the sound of the organ, and also the smell of incense. I love small, dark churches, and when I'm there I don't pray, but I indulge in a different kind of fantasizing, trying to solve problems that I don't really have the power to solve. For example, I think about the mystery of death and the future life and about God, whom I don't believe in as we have been taught, but who, I feel, exists inside and outside of me."

The fact that she was religious in her own way also seemed to please the man.

"I can dance, too," she added, thoughtfully, a little wary, for fear he would laugh at her.

He had turned again to look at her, and now he saw her in profile, and that face with its delicate and mellow colors, reddish and orange, against the background of green and blue daubs, illuminated by the reflection of the water, aroused in him an almost artistic pleasure.

And suddenly he also felt his heart seized with joy. She could be his. She was already his if he wanted her, that beautiful woman, pure and rich as a masterpiece.

"Do you know music, too?" he asked, continuing with that same type of examination to which she so willingly submitted.

Then she blushed and gestured "no," and he didn't insist in order not to humiliate her, for he well knew, before she herself confessed it, that her father had always been a simple master-mason. Building speculations made by the tough cunning of mountain people, and secret usury, were the source of her wealth.

But she, slender and straight as a hothouse flower, had nothing to be ashamed of, and she recovered herself, resuming almost with pride: "My childhood and even a good part of my adolescence were sad and rough. I grew up without a mother, and I came down here with my father like a pebble swept away by the falling rocks on the mountainside. Luckily, I found my relative, already established here for a few years, who has, in her own way, been sort of a mother to me, but more out of a sense of duty than out of affection. She was the one who nursed my father through his last illness as though he were a brother, and for that most of all, I am fond of her and respect her, and maybe also fear her. She is a severe woman, a little strange, who doesn't want others to enjoy themselves because she has never enjoyed herself. She exercises family dominion over me, because in our tradition, the elders still govern the young. I, who could be as free as a bird, am not free at all."

"None of us are free, and we are all to some degree slaves of our family."

"I am, after all, a carefree and unconventional person," she resumed, trying to affect an air of gaiety. "I am not afraid of life. I am not afraid of anything. On the contrary, I would like to take risks and face dangers in order to overcome them. I always think that something unusual will happen to me. And perhaps my desire is beginning to come true."

But when he did not answer immediately, as if confirming these words, she carried on. "Reality is different," she said, as though to herself. "Life is so flat, so monotonous, and people are all alike, each one focused on his own interest, especially material interests, that it is impossible to do anything but withdraw into oneself and live in dreams."

"You talk like that because, until now, you have only met such people, so you have created around yourself this rather superficial reality. But there are those, yes, thank God, there are those who think differently. You," he said, with a mildly bitter tone, "have not listened to my words. I don't mean to say that you didn't believe them."

"No, no," she answered emphatically, waving her arms within the wings of her cape with the movement of a captured butterfly. "You didn't listen to my words either. I already believe everything you say. But I've only known you such a short time."

"It's up to you to get to know me. Will you? Will you? Look at me."

They looked at each other again, the piercing, warm accent of that last '*will you*' had set her afire like a plea for love. Her lips swelled with the desire for a kiss, but the man thought it was still too soon.

When, after the long conversation, she shuddered dreamily, remembering that she was supposed to return home, the ashen shadow of twilight grazed her soul.

"I have to go," she sighed, bending down to look here and there as though she had lost something. No, she had everything:

the gloves still open and warm in her hands, the blue-beaded bag whose gilded opening revealed an interior as fragrant and colorful as a garden. Nothing was missing, and yet she had the impression that she had lost something.

She had lost herself behind a dream that already aroused in her a sense of risk and fear.

She stood up, and he grasped only her fingertips to bid her farewell and to keep her there longer. He looked up at her, his face close to her arm, his eyes reflecting the sadness of the twilight.

"When will we see each other again?"

"When? I don't know," she said, uncertainly. Then she left it up to him. "Whenever you wish."

"Tomorrow, then."

"Not tomorrow, not tomorrow." It seemed she was afraid their bond would too quickly tighten.

"Tomorrow," he insisted, laying his face against her arm. "Every day that passes is lost. I will wait for you here. I will not leave this place until you return."

She laughed faintly, but she felt his breath penetrate the fabric of her dress and warm her flesh, and she could not tear herself away until he eagerly stood up like a child who has found the solution to a problem.

"I'll come and get you."

"No, please don't come for now," she said quietly. "I'll be back here at the same time in three days."

And after he kissed her fingers to thank her, she walked away lightly, drawing into her cloak all the soft reddish-gold colors of the sunset, so that the cloak itself seemed to dissolve into the horizon of the garden at the end of the avenue.

Then the man headed back to the lake, already dark in the dark ring of holm-oaks, and his eyes spoke with the mystery of the water that reflected the mystery of the evening.

Did he really love the woman already? He desired her, of course, for she was beautiful, fresh, still unknowingly sensual. And he thought about marrying her, but would he have thought the same had she not been the woman he had deliberately gone to find?

"I will not conceal from you that I am rather indolent, if not lazy," he said to her when she returned, as if she had simply gone round the garden and he had actually stayed there waiting for her. "My nature is somewhat contemplative, but externally contemplative, I might say, because while I enjoy, perhaps to the point of ecstasy, the lights, colors, movements, and transformations of people and things, most of the time as I contemplate them, I remain just as focused on myself. Only rarely do the landscape and the environment of my soul merge with the landscape and the environment around me. I have so many things of my own to think about," he resumed, as she listened with silent and almost religious curiosity. "I have so many problems to solve that I do not like to concern myself too much with those of others. Therefore, I like to contemplate and think and move as little as possible. That's why I hate going among crowds. I like the carriage more than the automobile, and I love the warm, soft corners of drawing-rooms where intelligent men discuss things that interest me while the colors of fine, beautiful women contrast with those of flowers and paintings. You will say to me, 'In short, you are a pleasure-seeker and a real egotist.' Perhaps I am a pleasure-seeker, if you mean the pleasure of the spirit, but an egotist, no. Certainly not. I'm not capable, for example, of making even an animal suffer, not even a flower, for my own enjoyment. On the other hand, if passion moves me, I am ready to make any sacrifice. Not to boast, but, in the war, I silently did my duty with no other aim than to do it."

He spoke in a cold and colorless voice about the everyday moments and the tragic events when he had gambled his life like children flipping a coin.

She listened attentively, eagerly, but a shadow of worry veiled her eyes.

The weather, too, was somewhat strange: the air was heavy, though clear, like clothing no longer appropriate for the season. The lake, the light, the trees, and the circle of sky above them had a bluish-green tint. The dead flowers bent low, and a sense of decay infused everything.

And the things the man was saying seemed to deepen that sick feeling.

"What's wrong with you today? You seem sad. Is your relative sick?" he asked, looking at her, a bit dismal himself.

He did not miss the fact that she tightened her lips to prevent an uncertain smile, caused perhaps by the suspicion that he had asked that question ironically.

"My aunt is fine. She is a strong woman, who even knows how to overcome her own illnesses. She immediately noticed that something unusual was happening to me. So, because I like to be frank, I told her everything, and she is not happy."

"Why isn't she happy?"

"Well, because she says that there is too much distance between us. Your origins are too high and mine are too low, and the signs of class cannot be erased. You say so yourself. The roots are the tree's greatest strength."

"Love," he said sadly, "is the only root of life. Of course, if you do not love me, as I already feel that I love you, we will never be able to understand each other."

"That's what I'm most afraid of. I'm afraid of falling too much in love and suffering."

"Maria!"

Already that name, spoken for the first time — spoken with reproach, gratitude, and tenderness — quivered with the undercurrent of passion. And she shuddered, as if suddenly called from afar by someone painstakingly searching for her in the dark.

A veil of silence enveloped them, intertwining them, as if they had actually met in the dark and clung to each other, naked souls, free of all the impurities that divided them in the light.

"After all," he resumed, "I would not like you to be swayed by what I have told you and what I said to you recently. I would not like you, in short, to think me a great gentleman or a degenerate. I am a good man, after all, and I like the good life as all healthy and intelligent young people do. I'm a dreamer, but at the right time, I'm also a man of action, and like all indolent people, very active. Before the war, soon after graduating, I opened a law office, and it proved successful. I still have this small office in the countryside, and if I am here, it is because I want to expand my reach, work, and earn money. I want to have my own house, a family, and a safe place in the world. I had come to you that day, if you remember, to purchase the land where I planned to build a house. For," he added with the warm haste of a lawyer concluding an important defense, "below where you live there is a whole new city to conquer and control."

Again, silence gripped them, but this time it was hostile and ambiguous. They both thought, with longing and bitterness, that there was already a fine house to offer the man who, like a bird in love, wanted to build his nest. Offended by his own instinctive desire and offended by her because she was guilty of guessing that desire, he resumed forcefully.

"I will have everything I want, because what I want is simply human and owed to me. Our fathers, mine and yours, died young — mine from having enjoyed himself too much and yours from having wanted too much. And the shadow of their anxieties, and to be clear, their ignorance of laws and of life, still weighs on us. But I want to free myself of this shadow. I want to enjoy life, but only as far as nature allows, and to desire, but without effort, with patience and restraint. When I'm fifty, I'll be at the peak of my youth, astride life. I want to dominate and conquer it myself, this life that we think of as an external thing but that we must, instead, enclose within ourselves, making it part of who we are. Do you understand?" he said, turning impetuously, his face clearing, happy to have expressed himself well and definitively.

And she was almost afraid, afraid of losing him, of no longer counting for anything in his straightforward and clear future. How could she get him back? She felt that she had offended him by telling him about her rural aunt's judgment, and above all, by showing him that she was not completely free and outside the confines of her class. She too thought of defending herself with an instinct to get back at him that sent words into her mouth as cold and sharp as the flukes of an anchor. "I believe, feel, and think as you do, but I am a woman, and there is little I can do. I told you my aunt's opinion in order to clarify everything between us. I won't hide the fact that this woman exercises a certain power over me. As I told you, I don't feel I love her, but sometimes I admire her. She is a woman of character, a woman who thinks. She does not know life, but she intuits it in an extraordinary way. She sees things in a raw but precise light, and she judges and foresees everything with mathematical coldness. In our case, she may be wrong. Besides, you'll say, 'What do you care about this woman?' It is true. I am not dependent on her. I am completely free. And yet there is an almost mysterious fact that unites me to this woman, as to the root of our family, a fact that is partially unbelievable and symbolic, while also being extremely material. I am telling you now and beg you to believe my every word as if I were on the verge of death. So," she resumed after an anxious moment of silence, "I must tell you that my father died tragically. He fell from the ledge of a factory that was being inspected, and his death was atrocious. His body was completely broken, but his soul survived intact. His death throes went on. This relative of ours nursed him to the end, promising him that she'd watch over me. Then he, who, in the face of death, had become once more the straightforward and simple man of the mountains, gave her a necklace, which he had received as collateral — I do not yet know from whom — for a loan of thousands of *lire*. The necklace is made of pearls and very valuable. Well, this woman undertook to keep the necklace until the creditors came to collect it, or until the credit expired, which was fixed at no more than thirty years. I think twenty years have already passed. In another ten years, if the creditors, who, it seems, have a legal guarantee, do not appear, the necklace should be mine. But how can I be sure that this woman will give it back to me? She keeps it hidden, and she assures me that the creditors or their heirs will show up because every day the value of the pearls increases. If I disgust this woman, if she turns away from me, or I from her, what will happen? I must tell you something else.

"From the beginning, she kept the jewel at home, hidden, and I think she got into the habit of not going out for fear that it would be stolen. Sometimes at night, when no one could see her, she would fasten the necklace to keep the pearls alive. Well, I used to peek through the keyhole to try to see her, but I couldn't. I spent my adolescence dreaming about that necklace. I never asked for it, but I always thought about it, and at night, I dreamt about it. And it seems like a dream, something that happened ten years ago. I was already almost fourteen, but I looked older, and men in the street were already speaking words of love to me. All the turmoil of spring was stirring me, and one day, when my aunt had gone down to see the tenants of the cottage, I went into her room, searched, and in a very ordinary place, under the mattress, I found a leather case. I opened it easily and inside found the necklace. I joyfully put it on, and imagining myself at a great celebration, I tried a few dance steps. She surprised me and beat me ferociously. I hold a grudge against her for this as well. Afterwards, I believe, she put the necklace in a safe deposit box at a bank. Well, this necklace unites me to her, not so much because of my desire for it, but more because of the question whether, in due course, she will give it to me. I have no document that can prove my ownership. It all depends on my aunt's goodwill and familial honesty. My aunt feels that I do not love her, and perhaps, more than anything else, she dominates me this way in order to keep me tied to her. But perhaps the time has come to free myself."

When she had finished speaking, she looked at the man in a daze. She regained control of herself, realizing, however, that he too looked troubled and shaken. He looked at her as one looks at the mentally ill to give them the illusion of believing them sane.

With a swift and sure movement, she pulled the cloak she had let hang loose over her shoulders and clasped it at her throat, grimacing with the effort. He, in turn, felt that a careless word would be enough to offend her and make her go away, so he said, "You are still the child seeking the necklace as the symbol of life. When we are young, we dream of life as a party in a big city where the richest people in the world come together, and we would like to be the richest of the rich, the king of the party. Adolescence is the saddest of our seasons precisely because our instinct tells us that none of what we dream will come true, or worse still, that, instead of a party, a solemn beating awaits us. Your aunt, I have no doubt, will give the necklace back to you. In the meantime, you must truly free yourself from your family's prejudices and views.

Face life as it is. Decide your own destiny. I would also like to tell you that life offers you its most beautiful, true necklace, one that fastens us to eternity. But I don't want to create poetry, and I don't want to pull at your heartstrings."

She opened her cloak again, with a gesture of abandonment, but also in order to breathe better. In her eyes one could see the shadows of those ready to throw themselves over a precipice. "I understand, yes: love. True love," she said in a raw voice. Then she bowed her head like the roses wilting around her under the weight of time.

Something struck the man deep in his conscience. "You are right," he said humbly. "The love I offer you now is not yet what you want, nor is it the love to which your beauty and goodness entitle you. The two of us here are still two strangers meeting by chance in this garden, trying to enjoy each other only for their fleeting pleasure. Everything can be good for enjoyment and pleasure, even deception, especially deception. It is the business, or shall we say the instinct, of a man and a woman meeting each other. But let us hope this is not true for us. Let us hope so."

He, too, sighed sorrowfully like a sick man tired of hoping for recovery, and then he spoke again. "Let me hope, especially for myself. I was sick before I met you, and perhaps I still am. Sick from bad dreams, from cruel ambitions, from an almost brutish concept of life. I wanted to conquer this life, at any cost, as though it were prey. I was like a starving, bleeding man desperate to feed on raw meat, and I didn't realize that the true seed of life was dying inside me. Let me tell you everything," he resumed, after a dark, fearful pause. "When you opened the door to me, the light through this darkness enveloped me. It was like the opening of the sky after the night. I felt, and you noticed, the same joy as a man lost in a forest who meets a fellow human who can put him back on the right path. Yes, of course, all this is already love, but not yet passion, the passion that burns and purifies and forces you to start life over again. But it is up to you to make it become so."

"What shall I do?" she asked, folding her hands in her lap and shaking her head, which remained bowed.

He turned to look down the boulevard, and since bad weather was approaching and throngs of gray clouds, agile as tigers, were rushing from the horizon, he saw that the garden had become deserted. Only in the distance, the reddish figures of carefree children twirled among the flower petals torn off by the first breath of wind. Then he turned and put his hand around the woman's waist, touching the satin-like fabric of her dress as if it were her bare skin, and she shuddered to her deepest core. When he begged, "Give me a kiss," she closed her eyes and turned deathly pale. But when she opened them again, after the kiss, everything seemed more alive than before, inside and outside her, everything changed, iridescent and upside down as though reflected in a soap bubble.

After that crucial meeting, the man remained alone in the garden threatened by the storm. Like a drunkard aware of his state, he was afraid to move, feeling everything twisting and struggling around him from the opposing forces tearing him apart inside.

The hand that had held the woman trembled, accompanied by the rustling of the leaves. To control himself he raised his hand, closed it, opened it, and finally placed it under his other armpit, waiting for everything inside and outside to become clear. He felt his blood roar with the wind: more and more clouds were rising on all sides, and the dome above the lake resounded with the murmur of trees like a cathedral on Good Friday evening when the crowds sing and weep over the pain of death and the hope of resurrection.

Under his jacket, he touched the document the woman had spoken about, the one in which her father declared that he had received the pearl necklace as collateral — from his own mother, who had introduced herself under her maiden name. Thoughts and worries, problems, scruples, temptations, and intentions rose to his brain like clouds over the lake, stirring up a whirlwind.

He knew that his mother had pawned the necklace at a usurious price for the salvation and honor of their name. Why didn't the speculating usurer reveal her name to these women? And why didn't you, he asks himself, immediately tell your own secret to the woman who revealed her secret to you? Why didn't you tell her that, after many years of dreaming about the recovery of the necklace, you came down to the city to retrieve it at any cost like a diver going to the bottom of the sea to fish out shipwrecked treasure?

And why don't you tear open your conscience and confess that, after all, the necklace is the thread you need to guide you toward the fortune required to return you to the lazy and refined lifestyle of your ancestors?

"In short," he said to himself brutally, "since fortune does not assist you in any other way, you have come to find and win over the speculator's daughter. So, we're even. And if God calls to you, in his infinite goodness, and arouses love in place of hatred, and perhaps even crime, what are you complaining about?"

But he did complain, along with the wind, the mangled branches, and the water moving in the lake. He wished the storm would erupt furiously and sweep him away too.

He thought of tearing up the document and scattering it in the wind. And he thought of running away, of never seeing the woman again, but he didn't move. He didn't take his arms from his chest. The instinct to save himself held him firm, and he felt that, with the document, he was defending his very heart, his very conscience. "Perhaps I really will be the man I described to you," he thought. "I will work. God will help me." At last, until the weather cleared, he collapsed weary onto the damp bench as though he were a wanderer at God's mercy, and in the evening, when it became cold again, the pearl of the new moon appeared in a shell of cloud.

One evening, the young woman came home later than usual. She hurriedly undressed and dressed again and ran into the dining room. The table was already set and her aunt, who was waiting for her on the terrace, a little tired, received her with a silent reproach.

She adjusted a few things on the damask tablecloth and waited for the other woman to move. And as the other woman did not move, she went round the table and round the room. Wings of joy carried her. All was light and happy in the world and in that dining-room, unsteady but harmonious with its greenish walls marbled in gold, its walnut furniture, brightened by tiled studs in whose liquid background swam grotesque fish and branches with imaginary fruits. The glass window of the terrace opened to the horizon where the blue outline of the mountains was lost in the reddish blue of the sky. All this reminded her of the corner of the garden by the lake, where the man had asked her to be his wife.

But why doesn't the woman on the terrace move? Her black figure clutters the horizon, and the young woman, looking at her fleetingly, has the impression that she is seeing her for the first time.

And, for the first time, something about that small, exhausted, and sagging figure appears tragic. There is something tragic in the floor-length black dress, in her very pale face with its pained, closed mouth, her eyes hidden behind large purple eyelids and, above all, something in her short, thick hair, black on one side and white on the other, puffed up on her forehead with two rebellious bows, hair that tends upward like flame, continually breaking free from the hairpins meant to hold it down.

"Auntie," she said in a childish voice from the window, "aren't you coming? You're tired, aren't you? I'm late, aren't I? But I'll tell you why later. Shall we eat? Auntie...."

Her voice was childish, yes, and gentle, like children who want something; but her aunt knew that voice well and would not allow herself to be touched by its opportunistic gentleness. Instead, a jealous curiosity freed her to a certain extent from her hostile indifference.

"What happened to you?" she asked without moving.

The young woman went out on the terrace and leaned her back against the balustrade, almost trying to blend in with the enormous light of the sky to hide the flame that illuminated her from within. But everything betrayed her: the curly hair radiating around her face, against the red horizon, and her eyes, her teeth, her hands, even the trembling of her silver throat.

Her aunt felt as though she were next to a fire. Although it was a fire that did not touch her, it disturbed her. In the end, however, it was nothing but a grand illusion.

"Aunt, do you remember that gentleman, that Count Giovanni Delys, whom I spoke about some time ago, who came to see if the land below was for sale? Well, aunt," she resumed after a moment of uselessly hoping for an answer, but during which she felt that her aunt already knew everything, "a few days later, he wrote me a letter, a declaration of love. I did not tell you about it because it seemed to me a joke, a distraction. Well, in the last few days, I met this man again. He followed me and waited for me where he knew I was headed. And today, he finally comes up, asks permission to speak to me, tells me that his intentions are serious, that he loves me and wants to marry me. He is not rich, but he has enough to live modestly, and he is a true gentleman. I replied that I reserved the right to speak to you, and he expressed the desire to do the same."

"Speak to me? Why?" asked the woman immediately in a defensive tone.

"Aunt! You're asking me? And if we can't speak with you, with whom would we speak?"

"I am neither your mother nor your father, and you are old enough to understand what suits you."

"I have no one else in the world who can protect me. Also, as a formality, and so you can assess the man."

Then her aunt seemed to soften but still with a layer of hostility and distrust.

"You talk like the child you are."

He too had said as much to her. Since that is how she was judged, she forgave herself for the untruths she instinctively told in her own defense. "Then talk to me as you would to a child."

"In these matters, no one can see clearly, not even a father or mother, and any third-party intervention can lead to disaster. If I see the man, I will judge him according to my instinct, which is different from yours. What good can my opinion do you? You are free. You owe nothing to anyone. I can give you only one piece of advice: try to know the man well before you fall in love. If you love him already, you will never get to know him. It is all over," she then said, as she watched her niece bow her head. "You are already in his net."

"That's why I would like help. How can I know the man if I don't get close to him? And where can I get close to him if not here? And here, if you act distant and hostile, how can I receive him?"

"Have you asked for information about him?"

"Whom can I ask? It's something we should do together, the two of us. What reason, on the other hand, would he have to deceive me?" she asked, blushing. And she alone knew the reason for her blushing.

Her aunt had fallen back into a state of weary abandon.

"At other times," she said without warmth, "you have received declarations of love and marriage proposals, and you have never been so concerned."

"Because they didn't suit me. Now it involves an intelligent, noble, and handsome man, to say nothing of his situation. And, also, I like him. That's it: I like him." The sound of her last words resonated, sensual and provocative as a kiss. The other woman revived.

"That's it! And you're sure he likes you?"

"Yes, yes," she said with impassioned certainty. "I can deceive myself about anything but not about this. He loves me. He wants me. I can feel it."

"He's right. You're beautiful and young, and you love him. You're already in the net."

In spite of her exhilaration, the young woman felt a dull irritation at hearing such talk. It felt as if she were being slapped and that reality itself was speaking through her aunt's mouth.

"We are all in the net of illusion as long as we are alive," she said, unwittingly imitating her aunt's weary cadence veiled by sarcasm. "But imagine if it were not so. What would one live on? In any case, enough for now, we still have to talk about this business, but let's go eat now, aunt. I'm hungry."

And she seemed to want revenge.

But little by little, day by day, her aunt became convinced of the necessity of receiving the suitor in her house.

When the young woman went out, on those afternoons, already hot, full of dusty winds and the scent of gardens, which came from the west like the breath of the big city full of its passions and pleasures, her aunt felt a sense of unease and jealousy.

Alone in the house, she felt as though she were on a desert island. From the windows of the shiny and silent rooms, the sea, a glossy blue and iridescent green, seemed to overflow, and the undulating grass of the meadows and the orange curtain of the veranda, full and raucous as a sail, added to this impression.

The woman loved this bright solitude, but she felt lost in it, like a boat without a captain. What good was life to her? She loved no one, not even her companion who did not love her, and the days went by all alike, useless in their exasperating tranquility.

She wandered from room to room, creating for herself the illusion of doing something, until, tired from her worries more than from fatigue, she collapsed into the wicker chair on the terrace, rocking herself like a baby in its cradle.

Below, the land for sale revealed a miniature panorama with its thickets of nettles and broom, the paths, the embankments, the yellowish plains and lakes, the remains of the last storm. Sometimes, a flock grazed there, and the line of sheep stopping to graze one after the other on the grassy embankments augmented the sense of a vast, windy country. The land seemed once more to begin to live a pastoral life that wrenched the woman's heart with deep nostalgia.

She was born to live close to the earth with the grass and the snow, with the wind and the stones and the sun and the animals, to meet a man of her own class and start a family with him. Instead, life had thrown her into the city, into that shiny cage where only the wind brought her the voice of her distant homeland, of losses.

And she liked this nostalgia. It retained a sense of youth, of illusion, and therefore, of life. And she envied the young woman because she felt that, had a man like *that one,* who seemed to have come from a world of dreams or from a land of marvelous adventures, presented himself to her, her fate would have been different. She smiled, surprised to find herself still thinking about such things.

The quiet old man passing below on the road under construction, who stops and turns to look at the land, lifting his placid blue eyes to observe the little villa and the woman on the terrace — what would he say if he knew that the woman whose hair had already turned white was still thinking about love? But as long as a woman is alive and the light of her blood has not been extinguished in her flesh, what can she do but think of love?

The passer-by reaches the end of the street, as far as the hedge where the spiders are working and the baby birds are learning to fly. Then he comes back, one hand in his pocket, the other holding the strap of what seems to be a tobacco pouch slung over his square shoulders, his gaze remaining steadily on the woman. He is not as old as he seemed at first glance, but not young either: middle-aged, well preserved with a strong body that is still agile, a good height, comfortably dressed in English material. Wearing a white shirt with gold buttons at the wrists, he has a ruddy face with a dimple in his chin: the kind of man, in the end, that might suit her.

And a sense of warmth revives her; her heavy eyelids rise, as if relieved by that man's gaze. He certainly does not know who she is, and if he stares at her like that, it is perhaps because he likes her. Having passed the little villa, he turns to look at her again, then slowly, reluctantly turns away. But when he is out of sight, she sneers at herself again, and she again thinks that her body is on the verge of falling apart like an overripe fruit and that the gray twilight of life has already seized her by the hair.

And what about her niece who has not come back? An ugly surge of resentment, almost of hatred, again stirs her. She has the impression that the young woman is stealing something from her, that she has taken too much of the best of her life, or at least that there is an unjust imbalance between her, who has nothing, and the other woman, who has everything. And she thinks, finally, about the business of the necklace. She has known for a long time that it is the only chain uniting them.

Then she sneers a third time and is saddened by her mistrust. There it is, the poisonous cup she has always drunk from. Why not believe? Why not love? Why not love just to love, outside of oneself, outside of her miserable flesh? Love has as many rays as the sun, and the more it is outside the flesh the more perfect it is. The other woman will have children one day, and loving life again through the life of a child is greater than loving a man.

Tears of tenderness, sweet because they were tears, refreshed her large, burning eyes, and it felt as though a child who really loved her, who finally loved her because she loved him, was laughingly throwing handfuls of pearls against her face and chest.

The west wind ceased. The excited voices of nature in love ceased.

And beyond the blue silence that flooded the house, the voice of the city could now be heard. It was like the buzzing of the fever that stuns the sick person after sunset: a murmur of weary delirium, a ceaseless whirling in a labyrinth with no exit. There were cries, sounds of bells, whistles of sirens intertwined in a suffocating spiral. There were vibrations of anvils and a rumble, the rumble of a human river squeezed between the banks of heaven and earth. Gradually the noise took on a harmonious and solemn tone. It sounded like an orchestra with a thousand instruments, and it played the symphony of good and evil, of the sorrow and joy of the big city. And it was accompanied by a chorus of pilgrims on their way to the promised land.

At last, her niece returned. She fluttered about, a little bewildered, here and there, like a baby bird that failed in its first flight and accidentally entered a house. Then, after looking through the window, silently anxious, she softly said, "Aren't you coming? It's ready."

Her aunt did not move. She sat, hands clasped in her lap, her face lit by the reflection of the already moonlit sky. Was she praying? Was she sleeping?

A terrible sorrow and hope resounded in the voice of the other woman.

"Auntie? Auntie?"

"What? I'm not dead, no!"

"I called you twice. What's wrong?"

"Nothing. I'm coming now, but first tell me why you are so late."

And since she understands from the severe tone of these words that the moment to tell the whole truth, the moment she has been waiting for, has come, the young woman falls to the ground, like one who can take no more. "It's time to tell you, yes, where I've been. It's time," she sobs, pressing her hand to her forehead to stop her thoughts. "I've been out with him, with that man. And he persists in his marriage proposal, and he wants to talk to you. It's unavoidable."

"But is it really unavoidable? Why?"

The young woman bends further, almost as if to curl up, not from an instinct of self-defense, but to prepare herself so that her aunt, once she discovers the truth, can shun her and kick her far away.

"Listen to me. I told you that one day he came looking for you about the land. I opened the door, and he asked, 'Are you Signorina Maria Baldi?' I answered that I was. Isn't my name Maria Baldi? Maria Baldi is my name, just as it is yours. He had mistaken me for you. He still believes that I am the rich Maria Baldi and doesn't know that, instead, I am simply your beneficiary."

The aunt opens her eyes wide as if to listen better. Eventually, she laughs, but against her will, as though tickled.

"What sort of man is he? An idiot?"

"Oh, far from it," says the weeping voice.

"But excuse me, is he so stupid that he doesn't gather any information and makes such a mistake?"

"That's how it is, aunt, that's how it is. Why should he try to get information if I'm the one who convinced him to believe what he believes? I am the one who told him that I am Maria Baldi the mistress and not Maria Baldi the servant. Don't laugh, aunt, don't laugh; it hurts."

"Maria!"

"Yes, yes, don't protest, and don't be offended. What am I but your servant? What have I done, and what do I do for you, if not what the least of servants does? You took my poor father in and nursed him when he fell from your building, and at least, you let him die in peace by promising him that you would keep me with you as a daughter. And you did for me what you thought was your duty. Now I, on the other hand, have even stolen your name, just as on that day when I wanted to steal the necklace from you."

GRAZIA DELEDDA

"My God, my God," the woman said with a deep sigh. A crimson flush lit her face, which then became whiter. "Stand up," she said harshly, "you still have time to tell the truth."

"I even made him think that the necklace was mine — even the necklace! At first it was like a game, an adventure. I just wanted to see what the man is like. Now it is a tragedy, because I love him, and I cannot give him up. I am ashamed to tell him the truth. Even today I tried, but it was impossible. I want to die, aunt. Send me away, send me away; you will see that I know how to atone for my guilt."

"But what does he say about wealth?"

"He says nothing. He shows a perfect indifference to all material things that don't involve our love. And he says that if his income is not enough for the family, he will work. He wants to work. He has already decided to open a law office with another lawyer, a friend of his. I am unsure, however, whether, once he really knows me, he will still want me. I am sure that he came looking for you, but I am also sure that now he loves me. What shall I do? Tell me what to do!

"We should break up, I know," she resumed, changing her voice, as if the other woman were answering. "Tell him the whole truth at once, but that's it. I haven't the courage, and breaking is just a word. Today you break up, tomorrow you are back together again, and we're still here in a situation that's painful for everyone."

"Get up," demanded her aunt, who had, with indignance, already overcome her inner turmoil. "Let's not exaggerate. It is an experience like any other, and it is not the first and will not be the last time that a woman tries to deceive a man and vice versa. I think it will be good if you talk to him yourself, and right away, too."

But the mere idea of unmasking herself in front of him seemed to throw the young woman into a fit of madness. She didn't rise.

On the contrary, she curled up more tightly and began to moan from an almost physical pain.

The other woman let her calm down a bit, then resumed. "But how is it possible for you to reveal yourself to me now, but not possible for you to reveal yourself to him?"

"You know me. You know what I am. You can still beat and humiliate me without killing me. And you can also understand and pity me. This is a defining moment in my life. It seems to me that I am at the bottom of an abyss but that I can still be saved if you give me a hand. But with him, with him — no — I can't do the same. You are the one who must speak to him, partly because it is necessary for my conscience that you and he know each other."

And suddenly she raised her face, red with weeping, and looked boldly at her aunt. Her aunt, pale and unable to hide her revulsion, did not look at her. Then she rose, a little dazed but relieved, as though after a fainting fit.

"You heard me, aunt: *he came looking for you* that day, and now he must find you."

The woman laughed again, a laugh that lit up her whole being and made her teeth sparkle as though they had been restored to their original state. And her eyes became beautiful, to the point that her niece looked at her with surprise, and reflexively brightened as well.

But it was a flash. The shadow, thicker than before, returned to surround them. The young woman, however, as if invaded by a sense of cruelty towards herself, said, "You are laughing, aunt, but you know that if he saw you like this, as I see you now, he might prefer you to me."

Then her aunt stood up and said, sadly and ironically, "Let's not get theatrical, and don't make fun of me either. And if you really have this great trust in him, and you're both in such a thick web of deceit, it's better to break up definitively."

"Passion itself, as you once said, and life itself, are a web of deceit. One must die to get out of it. I, for my part, promise not to lie any more, but I feel that I have committed a sin and that I must atone for it, and perhaps this will be a good, not a bad thing, in my life."

"I don't know; I don't understand these things, and it hurts me to think about them. I like clarity, and perhaps that's why I've spent my life alone. At any rate," her aunt added wearily, as if to relieve herself of an annoyance, "if you think it best, I can even talk to him."

She received him the next day. In the large, bright, and cool drawing room, the windows open to the blue so that their diaphanous curtains fluttered, creating a sense of expectation, she did not hide from herself the fact that she was waiting with trepidation, curiosity, and a desire for revenge. Revenge for his being the man who had come to somehow skew the straight line of her everyday existence and mostly because she felt that she too might involuntarily be swept away in the drama of those two who said they loved each other yet were mutually deceiving each other as though at a masked ball.

Immediately, in fact, as soon as he entered, tall and confident, bowing to kiss her reluctant hand, smelling the scent of refined masculinity rising from his soft hair and from the bare nape of his neck, she felt a physical disorientation as if he were blowing on her fingertips the breath of desires that had led him to her. The man had not yet raised his head, and she had already become more hostile than before.

"Sit down."

He sat down facing her, his body seeming to follow the lines of the chair as though it had been tailor-made for him, his feet firmly on the ground, the back of his neck clinging to the swollen velvet of the high-back chair. With a certain expression of abandonment in his hands, he touched the knobs at the top of the armrests without grasping them. Even his face and gaze were calm, though a little fatigued, with a fatigue that has finally found rest.

"You think you are at home already," thought the woman with fierce derision. Yet, in the end, she was almost afraid that she would have to cruelly disillusion him.

"Signora," he began slowly, a little distracted, looking for the words he had already prepared and could not immediately find, "you already know the purpose of my visit. It was by chance that I became acquainted with your niece, Maria. More than her beauty, the expression of goodness and intelligence that illuminates her face immediately seized me and won me over. I allowed myself to follow her, to try to approach her and get to know her, and my most fervent wish is now to be able to become her companion for life." Encouraged by the impassivity of the woman who listened to him as if it were a financial affair, he resumed more attentively and rapidly: "I know that the young lady has no other relatives here but you. By her express and rightful wish, and mine as well, I have, therefore, thought it right to ask you for the honor of this conversation, first of all to get to know you and introduce myself, and then to ask if you have anything against the union of your niece and myself taking place as soon as possible." After a slight pause, during which he glanced fleetingly towards a window as if the rustling of the curtain aggravated him, warning him of something hidden, he continued, speaking even more slowly, "Your niece must have told you that I am not rich, but I have enough to live modestly and a profession that will help me increase my fortune." He did not continue. On the contrary, he frowned, almost regretting having said too much.

Then she spoke, lowering her eyes so as not to share in the sad impression her words must have made on him, but also a little disdainful at that involuntary, proud frown of his. "You're right. My niece is a good, simple girl, still almost a child. She doesn't know life yet and, like children, acts as though guided by fantasy and a desire for the imaginary. Or at least that's what she has done until yesterday. Yesterday, however, something happened in her consciousness, which suddenly opened up like a flower, and here I am, entrusted by her with a revelation whose consequences I cannot predict. Whatever they may be, at any rate, I am here and ready to accept them for everyone. I must tell you, then, that my niece comes from a humble family. Her father, a cousin of mine, was a simple and poor mason, and died as a result of a fall from a factory. I nursed him through his agony, and I let him die peacefully, promising to keep his orphan child with me and treat her like a daughter."

The man, in his turn, waited for her to continue, and since she did not continue, a dizzying bewilderment, like that which the mason must have felt when he fell from on high, made his mind go blank. His body bent, his face lost its composure, but quickly regained it, and he lifted his face to look at the woman, afraid of her.

She did not look at him. Then he examined himself quickly. He felt like a traveler who, after arriving at a comfortable place where he could rest at last, is instead immediately compelled to set out again. He felt as if he were being tricked by that pale and cold woman, who did not look at him to make him understand that she saw everything within him — tricked like a dream by reality. But the instinct for revenge and defense rekindled his strength and readjusted the mask to better fit his face.

"I love the young lady," he said in a hard voice, "and I do not take into account her origin or her material conditions. I am only sorry that she thought it necessary to put on a costume that was not hers in order to please me more. Not with her name, we hope."

"No, not with her name," answered the woman in a voice as distant as an echo. She looked at him with infinitely sad eyes. Then she said, "You are a noble young man, and I shall certainly be happy to consent to your wishes, but it is only right that we should speak plainly and understand each other well from the beginning. What my niece did is anything but worthy, and she understands and perhaps regrets it more than necessary. Her actions must be well evaluated, morally and materially, before making a decision that may be fatal to everyone." After a moment's waiting, she seemed to resolutely take her niece's side, almost as though to defend her from his generosity, perhaps more apparent than real. "But we must not forget the essential. After all, I have a good explanation for poor Maria's strange behavior. When she found herself in front of a person as distinguished as you, she thought she could raise herself to the same level with a lie created more from vanity than deception. When true love touched her heart, the mask fell and fell so hard that the wretched girl no longer had the courage to present herself to you as she really is. You must, therefore, pity her and, if possible, forgive her, but not impulsively as you now want to do. Think it over. You, too, are young, and you must not act on your first instinct, however generous it may be."

The man bowed his head as if actually reflecting, and he looked humiliated and sad. His face, however, again took on those furrows of plowed ground that aged him and refuted the woman's words then and there. She then felt bewildered and searched her conscience to try to resolve the fate of those two who, in the end, loved each other. What is to be done? Truth alone can save our conscience in ambiguous moments, so she resumed in a quiet voice, "And maybe the girl didn't think she was lying at all, because she hopes to inherit from me. And I would be obligated to fulfill her wish, for I brought her father from the village to build a factory in my building, and so I skewed his fate. Without me, he would not have died in that way, and the girl's life would have taken another turn. Aside from this, which may be a superstition, she is, in reality, my only direct heir. And she can especially count on the necklace, because her poor father actually did get it from someone who promised to take it back by a certain date. And he, who was a businessman but also a man of conscience, left it to me with the promise that I would pass it on only after my death, to my direct heirs, always with that same promise, if it was not reclaimed in time. And so far, I repeat, my only direct heir is my niece. Let me speak," she insisted, observing a gesture from him of almost anguished protest. "It is necessary. Life is difficult, and one must look life in the face. I don't know what may happen to me tomorrow. I may fall ill, but I may also find the opportunity or the need to create a family. Am I old? Am I young? I don't know. Sometimes I think I am close to death. Sometimes I feel a deep instinct to live. One does not marry just to love, and loneliness is terrible when one has no material concerns."

"Our family will be your family," said the man in a troubled voice. He immediately regretted these words, because the woman instinctively became distrustful with a distrust that went beyond the material things they were discussing, but which he, affected by his conscience, interpreted another way.

"Your family will be your family," she said sadly. "Everyone must have his own home and hearth." Then she shuddered, leaned further back into the corner of the sofa, and her gaze brushed over the things surrounding her as if to make sure they were in place, still all hers. Everything was fine, everything was hers, and no one could take anything from her without her permission.

"So, we must understand each other. One day, the girl can have everything, but that does not depend on me. It depends on the circumstances of life, and life is not in our hands. I can't commit to anything today."

Then he, completely offended, raised his head.

"Signora, please don't insist on this. I don't want anything. I completely understand what you're trying to tell me. You mean to tell me that my possessions will not be enough to live on. That will depend entirely on us. And if they are not enough, I repeat, I will work."

"Work, too, is difficult today."

"I will work," he adamantly repeated. And a surge of pride as well as faith, impelled him to reveal his secret and to cry out to the woman who had inherited from her father the lower class's instinct for avarice. His hope was to buy the necklace back from her, money for money, since that's all she thought about.

But he thought she *knew* and was waiting for him in ambush to better overpower him. Be quiet, he said to himself. If from day to day, from trial to trial, you feel more like a man, be quiet and work. And he rose up, great and imperious before her.

"Tomorrow," he said, his face re-assuming a virile hardness, "if you will allow me to come back, I will bring you the documents that prove my financial standing. From the vast estate lost by my father, among other things that generate little income, I have a large villa by the sea, completely rented in winter and summer. I keep an apartment for my own use. In town, I own another small house, where I have a law office, a practice that I plan to bring here and expand. If things should go badly, my family and I, should God allow me to have one, could live there. Love is enough to generate true wealth. Tomorrow, Signora, I'll show you the contracts."

She blushed so violently that he stopped as if struck by a cry.

"Forgive me," she murmured. Her tone was so sorrowful and kind that she felt her eyes fill with tears, and she remained motionless, her breath soft so as not to betray her agitation.

"It's your fault," he resumed in a low voice. "You don't understand that I'm a little lost here. I still feel like I did the day my mother died, and I thought I was alone in a desert. For this reason too, I left my solitary life up there and came down into the world in search of company. Has fortune helped me? I don't yet know. You're right, one must first evaluate things well, but I'm not looking for fortune. I'm looking for love, tenderness, human solidarity. You are intelligent, and you must understand me."

She grew more and more rigid, her eyes hidden, and he felt desperate. Again, he thought, "She knows everything and thinks I am play-acting." And, again, he said to himself, "Be quiet and work." He only said, "May I, then, ask you for a definite answer?"

"If you wish, beginning tomorrow, you can come visit my niece here. I have nothing against doing as you both wish. But I repeat, think hard about what you are going to do."

He immediately wanted to ask her to meet with her niece. She wanted the same thing, and yet both remained silent.

She thought, "Tomorrow you may not come back." And he rose abruptly, hurt by having sensed this thought.

"Until tomorrow, then," he said, kissing her hand again.

And his casual manner of bidding good-bye and leaving made him seem to the woman like a man who has shed a burden and is glad of it, but who also wishes to escape without seeming to do so.

And, in fact, he was driven by an instinct to flee. He was afraid of that house, of its blue serenity, which turned green with the sunset and recalled the serenity of the sea before the storm. And he was afraid, above all, of the two women who now held him tight like the arms of a pair of tongs.

Flee! And he proceeded lightly along the wide road clear as a river, against a background lit with red fumes. Where was he? He felt as if he were lost and that he would have to walk a long way before finding his path again. But what was his path, after all, in that city where he had neither home nor relatives nor friends? All roads were foreign and hostile toward him, and all of them could become his if he wished. And he felt beaten by this quarrel that, through the paths of his veins, resounded in his blood.

And yet he seems to recognize that road, to have walked it at other times, as a child or in a dream. At other times, he has seen the gates of the gardens swollen with black ivy and the blot of trees diffused against the green of the sky and the villas closed as though enchanted in the sunset and the big cages where new constructions are rising. In front of one of these constructions, a mountain of broken bricks, which look like pieces of bleeding flesh, forces him to get off the sidewalk. Suddenly, from the loose earth and the rubble, a person leaps out and penetrates his heart.

A small lady, dressed in black, a little hunched over, moans softly. Why does she moan? Is it from fear of that difficult pass, or because of some secret sorrow of hers? She doesn't pay any attention to the man she meets, and she disappears on the other side of the brick mountain.

He thought of his mother. One day, like the small lady who bore an extraordinary resemblance to her, she must have passed along that street, also moaning, in search of the usurer. So lonely and fragile, she too was lost in those streets and in the cruel twilight of the new city.

GRAZIA DELEDDA

He wanted to accompany the mysterious woman, to ask if she needed help, but no matter how much he searched, he could no longer see her.

"Mamma, Mamma," he murmured like a lost child. And again with the instinct of the vagabond who had thrown himself onto the bench in the garden by the lake, he was about to sit on the bricks.

Meanwhile, the young woman went out onto the terrace and found her aunt waiting for her with a cold and mute anxiety. Only the girl's eyes spoke, rushing to meet those of her aunt with the supplicating anguish of someone about to be killed.

When she heard how the conversation had gone, and the man's promise to return, she sat down on the windowsill, with her face in her hands. "He won't be back," she said.

The older woman made no reply. Standing straight beside the balustrade, she lay her hand, which the man had kissed, on the marble, and she looked at that hand with a sense of derision. Her silence increased their mutual pain.

Suddenly, however, the young woman rose, shook back her hair, and said roughly, "Maybe it's for the best. At least everything will be over."

Silence again. And both seemed simply intent on looking into the meadow.

The flock was still grazing among the sheaves of broom. The gray herd of sheep made a silvery undulation against the light with rust spots on their backs and pinkish colors on their melancholy ears. The dog, who, perhaps out of his long association with the herd, had taken on the appearance of a lamb, snout on the ground, also seemed to be grazing. From time to time, he raised his head and let out a loud cry, clear above the dense bleating surrounding him, as though to remind himself of who he was.

And in contrast to that gentle undulation of beasts and vegetation, in an unpaved space nearby, a few boys with long legs, dressed in barbaric, blood-stained shirts, were shaking the air with cries of their struggle and the mad chase of a large ball that seemed made of lead and yet bounced lightly and silently, alive and happy to be the hero of the game. The swallows above were also weaving a dizzying dance, shrouding the stillness of the sky with the net of their flight and screeches. On the ground, reddened by the setting sun, long shadows of slender giants played on their own with their own black ball with no shouting or passion: an agile and imaginary game that the boys seemed to be coarsely imitating. And the shadows of the swallows danced in the middle like black leaves pushed by the wind.

Also, intent on the game and on the struggle of their own thoughts, the two women did not speak. But when the sun, the boys, the flock, and the swallows had disappeared, the older woman rose, soothed, feeling as though she had rested after a long walk, and she summoned her niece back.

They had to get back on course.

The man returned at the appointed hour. He stood, waiting in the sunny drawing-room where the curtains, shaken by the west wind, struck him as making hostile, mocking movements towards him. As though to appease them, he prepared devotedly to kiss the hand of the lady of the house, when his fiancée silently and hesitantly entered.

Though disturbed, he looked at her with curiosity. As she advanced unwillingly toward him, she looked ill as though someone were pushing her forward, her eyes full of fearful sadness.

He did not go to meet her but opened his arms to her as though to a child taking its first steps. And because she hid her face in her chest, her shoulders trembling, he said almost irritably, "Don't cry now, all right?"

She straightened at once. She wasn't crying, but her suffering face had the expression of someone twisting and cruelly breaking her own pain.

"That's good," he said, leading her toward the sofa where her aunt had been sitting the day before. He sat down next to her and asked in a low voice, "Where is your aunt?"

He seemed to be afraid of her aunt, as his fiancée was afraid of him, and this revived and brought them together again with a sense of friendly complicity.

"I don't know. She's in the other room. She'll come now," she said softly and hurriedly, looking at the wide doorway of the drawing-room. She waited a few moments, watching to see if anyone could hear her, then she spoke again in the same tone as before. "My aunt is outraged, very angry with me. She is right. And I haven't slept all night. I even got up. I came here. I thought you had stayed here to ask me for explanations. And we had a talk. You heard it, didn't you?"

Tired from already saying too much, he didn't speak. Words were now useless. Everything had been said. Now it was necessary to abandon himself to time, to the race of life. So, he embraced her, and she immediately felt revived by the living embrace of the flesh of his arm and by his hand grasping her to the core. And after so much useless thinking and so much useless suffering, she fell against him as an exhausted and chilled swimmer falls onto the warm sand after fighting the stormy sea.

In vain, she tried to resume the imaginary conversation she said she'd had with him during the night. "I felt you didn't want to come back, and I too wanted it that way. Isn't that right? We both put up a good fight last night, and yet here we are. Why? Why? Is it God's will? I feel as though I have descended into hell and have risen again, burnt but safe. I can even die of pain now. It doesn't matter. I'll even accept martyrdom if I can love you. But," she said, trying to break away from his eager and silent grasp, "there is still time. Perhaps it is better to break things off."

As a reply he holds her more tightly. He places a kiss on her neck, arousing throughout her body the luminous fragment of a shudder. And souls, withdrawn into their deep refuge, allow the flesh alone to speak its divine language.

Not far away, on the terrace, her aunt overheard this conversation and could not help being upset. She did not know what to do, whether or not to go and interrupt it. What did these fiancés think of her? They must have thought she was leaving them alone so that they might immediately clarify things and understand each other better. And this had indeed been her intention, but deep down she felt that they were glad she wasn't there and that they understood each other too well. This understanding of theirs, made of kisses, this finding each other outside of every other vain interest, pricked her with envy, almost hatred. She felt that her house itself was driving her out in order to better welcome the love of these two and partake in their happiness.

"He had come looking for you and believed that he loved you through me; he would have loved you had he seen you beautiful as love makes you." The words of the dreamy and repentant young girl again blew over her face with the fragrant wind from the bushes in the meadow. She looked down at the children playing and up at the swallows and the shadows, and thought that everything in life is play. Knowing that these two had fallen in love in her house, and hoped to own it one day, already enjoying it like beetles in a rose, crushed her to the core.

And driven by an instinct of rage and anguish, as if he had sinned against her, she rose and returned, stamping the floor to warn them of her arrival. The man, who had already sprung to his feet, went to meet her and kissed her hand with intensity; she felt that it was saturated with the other woman's scent.

She was the one who wanted the wedding to take place as soon as possible.

The information requested from his town's mayor was good. The papers needed for the wedding had arrived quickly. Everything was in order.

She provided the bride's trousseau and gave her jewels and money. As the day of the wedding drew near, she seemed to become more amiable, maternal, and full of care and kindness for the betrothed. But they, especially the man, were not deceived. She was in a hurry to send them away and be rid of them forever.

When they were gone, this hope seemed to transform into certainty.

Here, at last, she is alone in her house, which is now entirely her own, and the past falls back into the shadow of nothingness. That man, whom she hardly knew, as though during a short trip, has no more substance for her than a passer-by in the street.

After all, she was glad to have the girl well-settled, better than she had dared hope, and above all, to have fulfilled her duty. The promise she had kept, the security of the future, the tranquility of the present, almost gave her a sense of fullness, of sleepiness. All that remained was to lie down and sleep.

"Giovannina," she says to the no-longer-young, trustworthy, and silent servant, who walks about in her felt shoes and asks nothing but to please her new mistress, "be sure to close the shutters and the front door and the gate. You know that we are alone in the house."

The servant follows her orders. One can hear the screeching of the bolts and the gentle banging of the shutters. Only the window in the mistress's room is still open against the background of a dark starry sky. Along with the warm night air, it lets in a sad and quiet nocturne of distant piano music that suggests both prayer and self-reflection. The music seems to have been composed by a tired, old, religious musician thanking God for letting him live without joy, but also without sin, weaving his last song as the silkworm weaves the cocoon in which he encloses himself to die.

The woman, too, closes the window. She is finally alone with herself in the room whose rustic character she wanted to preserve with its lime-painted walls and its antique furniture, which reminded her of her hometown.

The lamp itself, mounted on a wrought-iron candelabra, was composed of three snakes, their hooked tails resting on the marble of the bedside table. Their heads stuck out from their struggling, twisted bodies, holding the ring for the candle in the middle. It is a funeral candelabra whose flame used to illuminate the peace of death following the struggle of life. She held it as a sacred object, and in saying her prayers while undressing, she addressed herself not so much to Christ on the wall as to the three serpents who, in that pause from their endless struggle, seemed almost alive.

And that night she lingers to look at them, her eyes shining with astonishment. Abandoned, tired, on the chair at the foot of the bed, she is unable to undress. She is afraid of going to bed, of turning off the light.

What is happening with the three black snakes this evening, moving on their shadows as though coming close to unknotting themselves and leaping to the floor at her feet to bite her? She instinctively withdraws her feet and makes the sign of the cross. But even prayer tonight has an ambiguous meaning, and asking God in his kingdom and through his mercy to turn away temptations, resonates more with her flesh than with her spirit. She thinks of those two who, at this time, lie twisted like the snakes of the candelabra. She flees from that thought in vain, overwhelmed by it like the third serpent.

Postcards and letters from the bride enlivened the early days of her arid solitude. The bride and groom traveled, till one day they stopped at the villa by the sea, as if the sea prevented them from going further. From there, she received a letter from him.

He wrote with almost paternal tenderness about his young wife, explaining that they had stopped there because she wanted to. Already, she was feeling a little tired and longing for a stable home life. "We are here in the highest apartment of the villa, above the boundless sea, lulled by the music of the wind that does, however, occasionally turn infernal. The beach is almost deserted aside from a broken-down building that looks like a wooden cross floating on the edge of the sea. It is adorned, at night, with brilliant electric bulbs and the fluttering of the nocturnal butterflies, who are the town's intrepid dancers. These girls love dancing so much that when they do not find any partner, they dance with each other. The sentimental music of a little band accompanies them, and each player keeps a flask of wine next to his chair. As the party progresses, after they play dance music and drink, the music becomes warmer and more exciting. When the wind isn't blowing, we, too, join them, and Maria enjoys herself there like the child she is, tacitly accepting her role as queen of the party because of her beauty and elegance.

"And for once we really did have a good time, but not more than once, as is true, moreover, in all life's parties. Here, then, one must admire the effort that men and women, especially the latter, exert in trying to show how much they know about the latest fashion in dress and dance, a fashion exaggerated indeed. If the Parisian ladies wear belts above the waist, here they have them lowered below their bellies, and the steps of the latest dances truly recall those of Salome. It's not the music of the slightly drunk little orchestra that gives these ingenious couples, putting on airs, the freedom to twirl, but the great music of the distant world carried by the imagination like the sound of the sea from a shell. In the end, we are all equal, for there is no truer truth than that the whole world is a village, and we are all villagers listening to the voices and calls of a world of joy and beauty that is beyond the ends of the earth.

"Some, desiring this kingdom with which there are no sure ways of communication, get lost like lonely children in a big city, or even worse, in a forest. Among others, there is a woman here who constantly wanders the beach and the avenues around the village, a former singer who had some success in provincial theaters, now mad and in the most complete misery. A few of her poor relatives give her food and a bed. She spends her days wandering but without ever passing through the village streets. From time to time, when she thinks someone's listening, she hints at a tune or begins a romantic poem, never going beyond the first notes or verses, as though she has forgotten the rest. Her pure soprano voice is still fresh and powerful.

"One day, Maria and I were on the sea in my little rowboat when we heard a marvelous voice sporadically coming from the land like a scent brought in by a breath of wind. I still didn't know about this woman, who had only been here a short time, so I began listening to her with the illusion that I was seeing her, tall and dark, standing straight in the midst of a flutter of blue veils that met the waves. And the waves approached the land to hear the song that competed with that of the sirens.

"We, too, were curious to see her. Moved, Maria recalled the chant of the nuns in the church where I followed her that evening of our first meeting. The same deep and harmonious voice, the same notes that rise from infinity to infinity and take our hearts away with a breath of vertigo, and finally, the same passion that overwhelms us and becomes our own passion.

"So, we drew nearer to the shore, but now the singing hushed, stopped, then resumed, increasingly dull and faded. The woman might have sensed our curiosity, but she seemed not to have noticed our arrival. She was at the top of the pier, and I shall never forget her small figure, an old barefoot beggar with her big, hard, gnarled feet and a black scarf tied under her sharp chin. Her bloodshot blue eyes, as though never closed, stared into an obscure distance. But what troubled us most was seeing her, every now and then, throwing herself on the ground, as though tired and wanting to lie down, and then, as if repelled by the earth itself, immediately bouncing back, and standing upright, facing the sea and again singing.

"Perhaps I am deluding myself. Certainly I am deluding myself, but I believe that she feels in her inner world the way I saw her through the sound of her voice: beautiful, young, dressed in blue. That platform of boards is the stage from which her passion spreads out over the audience of the sea, the only theater where she can find something of the infinite love, the infinite greatness, the impossible dream that has deformed her and closed her in this prison of madness.

"Almost all of us, after all, are like that. Our body is often a grotesque garment hiding the beauty and youthfulness of our spirit. If we lived blind, perhaps life would be better. We would meet and get to know each other better through the sound of each other's voices."

On the very day this letter arrived, a sudden need to change her life drove the woman out of the house.

"If anyone comes looking for Signorina Marietta Baldi, tell them that she is not at home. If they ask for Signora Maria Baldi, tell them that she is still out," she told the servant, who did not quite know why she was given this order.

Usually, she wanted to be called Signora. Now, she thought, she was taking a stand even with herself and establishing her true personality.

She was an unmarried woman, a *Signorina*. Elderly, but still unmarried, and deep down she always felt like Marietta, the little Marietta with two curls of brown hair sticking out on either side of her forehead like the tips of the new moon, the Marietta who went out to pasture the sheep.

"He wants something from me. Perhaps they have already run out of money," she thought as she descended the silent, spotless staircase, after ordering her servant not to let anyone in.

And the thought of answering doesn't worry her, because she doesn't want to answer. What did she care, in the end, about all that literature?

But when, on the street corner, she saw the tall beggar woman with the pale face and black eyes with their noble sadness, she recalled the figure artfully drawn in the letter. Perhaps this beggar woman had also been a great lady. She made a gesture of taking her change purse out of the bag she held tightly. Then she went on without giving anything. The beggar was a nuisance to her because she wandered outside her house all the time and often rang her doorbell, insistent and harassing. She was a beggar born a beggar, and the man who wrote the letter had composed that mosaic of beautiful words because he wanted something too.

"Marietta Baldi, go straight on your way, and remember the first man who, when you were a child, came after you, through the innocent grass, and said words as beautiful as the flowers around you and promised sweets and almonds if you would go with him behind the hill. Since then, you knew what men wanted and walked straight on with a stone in your hand, watched like your sheep by the fierce dog you kept on a leash.

We are what we are and what we prove ourselves to be. You, Marietta, don't get it in your head that you are an agile, beautiful girl, when you are already a heavy woman with hair that smells of ashes and feet that soon tire of walking, just because today you have the audacity to wear the shoes of a girl in love. Go and take the lucky coach that stands where the great streets of the city begin and hold tight to the purse with your one true strength, the one that never deceives."

But she had gone out to walk, to see people, and besides she distrusted coachmen. So, she walked as far as the big street where the long series of luxury shop windows begins in front of which someone always stands in religious observation. She stops too. Here is a shop displaying only one article of women's clothing. On the white velvet surface is spread, as if softly slipped off by a princess, a dress of blue tulle glittering with silver beads. Beside it lies the open fan that recalls little nocturnal clouds passing over the moon and a rose, the blue rose of legends. This symphony of blue gives the woman looking at it a vision of the sea, and a wave of joy and freshness washes over her despite herself.

But she recovers immediately and continues on. It is better to stop in front of the other shop window, where the fruits in the cornucopias, happy to contain them, look so artificial, so big and dyed with the most vivid and various colors, red next to gold, and violet next to emerald green.

Gold and ruby-red and gold and purple and green and white make up a majolica in the next window, the florist's, gladdening the eyes of the beholder. But it is also dangerous to stop here, for the scent of carnations in summer makes one think back to a voluptuous night or at least to the dreams of women on terraces festooned with stars.

Walk, walk, and do not stop any more, even in front of that brilliant firmament of all the constellations and all the colors of the rainbow in the goldsmith's window. Nothing you want is there, because none of those jewels is more beautiful than your own.

Yet she paused at the sudden revelation of what had driven her out of the house. At last, she knew where she wanted to go, and since it was a fairly distant place, she waited for the tram and got on.

And suddenly she felt happy. Sitting next to the open door, she could see the buildings and the gardens in an airy and fresh background. At times, a gust of wind blew through her hair, giving her the impression that the sea lay at the end of the road over which the tram slid with the imprudent speed of a little scoundrel, and something indefinably sweet refreshed her soul, her face, and the hands clutching her bag.

Never had the city seemed so beautiful to her, so much her own. She felt that she held it in her hand like her purse, and she looked without envy, indeed with joy, at the great palaces with their loggias, red with geraniums and carnations. She, too, had villas and land and money, and never had she felt as rich as on that day.

Suddenly, however, the tram stops, jolting the travelers and calling them out of the bliss of their comfort, and an uproarious crowd assaults it.

There are women and women, some painted like color lithographs, others pale with clusters of black hair against their gaunt cheeks, hollowed out as if by violent passions. Others, beautiful and fresh in tulle dresses that they seem to have been born in, are like dragonflies with their wings, and like dragon flies, they are variously colored and with long slender legs.

Where are they going?

They all seem willing to travel bravely through the city, pressed into the tram like fruit in a box, all headed for a party, all ready to dance.

The pleasure of venturing out, of having escaped the nest of their home, the snare of daily and sterile duty, is evident in them all.

Or is it she who thinks she sees these things, intoxicated by that smell of young flesh, overwhelmed by that wave of femininity that is moved only by the necessities of everyday life?

Now the roar of the city was coming from outside, along with the smell of the wet asphalt. The shop curtains swelled in the wind, as though to fend off the sun and prevent it from spoiling the things they sheltered. And the sun came back reflecting off the signboards, exaggerating their gold and enamel.

Silk-clad saleswomen appeared at the doors of the shops like princesses at the loggias of their palaces. Large bespectacled ladies crossed the streets amidst the danger of cars and carts, as calm as whales in stormy waves.

And all the women, gradually descending from the tram and mingling with the crowd, were just as confident and quick, all in their element, their eyes accustomed to danger and how to avoid it. In the end, she envied them, for despite her wealth, she did not possess the pulsing strength of their ankles or of their fingers, ready to grasp every flower and every hook.

Oh, to be like that! Life would not be as heavy and useless to her as the purse she held in her hands. Or maybe she was deceiving herself. What was in her heart that day? It was like on certain nights, after eating and drinking too much, when a feverish life comes into your sleep, tinging your dreams with exaggerated colors, and you want to wake up but can't.

When she reached the point where she had to get off, she hesitated a moment. All she had to do was not move and pay another fare to return home and resume her usual life. This was enough to wake her up. But as if in a dream stronger than her will, she got off and fearfully crossed the street. Then she was in the hall of a princely palace.

It was a bank lobby.

She descended cautiously down the little stairway that led to the marble vaults. Suddenly it was night. The cold white light of the electric bulbs illuminated the place, and snowy freshness gave the impression of being in a mountain cave.

Here is the first room, round, and with a circle of people at a long table as if intent on a game. Cards come and cards go. A man, seated in the midst of the others, leads the game. It is he, with a serious, long, and hairless face who controls, distributes, and withdraws the cards, his fine white hands, his purple nails pointed like those of a woman. Every gesture he makes is calm, slow, almost religious. It seems as if he's performing a rite, touching and handing over the cards like consecrated hosts. In fact, the others, too, hand them over and austerely receive them, without paying attention to anything but the cards.

When it was the woman's turn, she, too, handed over a yellow booklet. The man quickly looked at her face with a mechanical gaze. He recognized her at once, looked at the booklet, and handed it back.

Then an attendant dressed like the servant of a great house led her into a second room surrounded by little doors lined with metal. Opening one of these, he ushered her into a sort of cubicle, and with a numbered key, opened a metal door on the wall. Then he left.

She closed the door and found herself inside as if in a marble tomb illuminated by a white light that seemed to emanate from the walls. And everything seemed unreal to her in that silence where the noise of the city came as if from the depths of the sea that churns the waves on the surface. Her own hands and their shadows and the keys in their coded rings, like amulets, and the metal slab in front of her reflected her face like a mirror, a demonic face full of sinister sadness that seemed to look over the opening of a mysterious place where she was condemned to watch over a cursed treasure.

She opened and pulled down the slab, which became a shelf. From the inside of the alcove, like the alcoves of the underground cemeteries, she drew out a zinc box. With the smallest of the three keys in the ring, she opened this little coffin, and inside appeared the treasure: paper and paper. But as she removed the packages tied up with white ribbons, her fingers fished out a leather case from the bottom of the box and triggered its spring. And the glow of dawn shone through all that sepulchral white. On the red satin of the open case, the beads of the necklace laughed like teeth in a child's mouth.

On her way back, as she was getting on the tram, grasping the handle with one hand and holding her bag in which she was carrying the necklace, she met two blue eyes that seemed startled to recognize her. She, too, felt a sense of bewilderment. Where had she met those eyes that, in spite of their foxlike reddish lashes, held a childlike goodness?

And now the man, to help her remember, lightly touches his hat in an act of greeting. Then he sits down beside her.

It is the gentleman, already gray but still youthful and well-built, in the very fine, brown, loose-fitting suit, who she has seen passing back and forth, courting her land. She now has the impression that he wants to court her, too.

But he does not say a word to her. He only looks at her secretly, examining her from head to foot and back again. She feels that look, somewhere between naivete and malice, run over her like a spider's thread, but after moving across the surface of her dress and around her veiled head, his gaze turns to her neck, still marked by a youthful line under the chin, and is pleased by that slightly voluptuous furrow. Then, his look caresses the nape of her neck and a curl that has furtively escaped. Finally, it penetrates the neckline of her dress, and attempts to delve into it.

She turned her back abruptly on the intruder and looked out the window again, sheltering her bag against her side. Suddenly, she saw the uphill road open wide, as if on high ground. Above a garden wall, she saw a landscape of pines, cypresses, and roses against the background of the golden sky.

It looked like the walls of another invisible city, and she felt her heart ache and a desire to cry over the memory of the letter and over the impression that this was the unobtainable city she had sought in vain that day.

A few days later, her servant came to tell her that a gentleman was downstairs asking to be received. She already knew who he was, and she stood up quickly as if she had been waiting for him until that moment. "Ask him to come in and enter the living room," she said, barely looking at the calling card that the woman had handed her. Then, she went to her room and put on the necklace, letting the best part of it slip and hide inside her dress. She didn't know whether she was doing all this to look more beautiful or more wealthy. But the man paid no attention to the jewelry. He stood at the table, like the other suitor, and on seeing her enter, he blushed and bowed, a respectful and sincere bow that, however, struck her as farcical. His blush and awkwardness also made her mirthful, and there was something comical about his entire person, his clothing, and the way he moved. She thought that the character actor in her internal drama had perhaps come on stage.

"Have a seat," she said, pointing to the armchair in front of the sofa where she sat down. She had done the same with the other suitor.

The man took a seat, a little shyly and awkwardly, without leaning against anything. He seemed afraid of sinking, partly because his short legs did not allow him to completely touch the floor.

She was still thinking of the other man, who had taken that place with the confidence of a conqueror, and she felt the screeching inside herself like the music of a forgotten instrument. It was an outburst of mockery for everyone and everything, for that other man, for this one, and, above all, for her, who was performing a play for herself.

The new suitor began with almost the same words as the other man.

"You, of course, Signorina, will guess the purpose of my visit."

That "of course" reminded her of the tragic sense of the scene. This man was sincere and lucid, his mere presence, like a primitive being with no awareness of his own awkwardness, made her laugh. Since she did not answer, he was reinvigorated and resumed.

"The other day, I wanted to take advantage of running into you to speak with you, but I did not dare. It was not the right place, and please excuse me if I allowed myself to greet you. However, I realized that you had already noticed my very humble person, as you have undoubtedly seen me more than once walking around, precisely here on your grounds. I have been courting your land for a long time, Signorina, but I know that you still have no intention of selling, and I approve of that. You possess capital that increases day by day. However, it is not about that now. It is, Signorina, you understand, about the fact that I like you very much and am glad to be able at last to express my feelings to you."

She kept silent, passing her handkerchief over her forehead as if to wipe away the sweat from real work. She had become serious and stiff. She didn't know why, but an almost tragic sadness darkened her soul, as though not she, but someone, who held her in his power, was forcing her to determine her fate by listening to and agreeing with the words of her suitor. And he shuddered at the expression of her earnestness.

"Signorina," he resumed, relapsing into his earlier uncertainty, "do not misjudge me, and do not think me too simple or odd if I proceed in this way. Another man would have acted differently. He would have had someone recommend him to you and would have tried to get to know you better, and for you to know him better, before making a declaration. I'm an informal man, and

I don't know how to stand on ceremony. I judge and let myself be judged according to feelings. I am also a bit of a fatalist. I let myself be guided by destiny and close my eyes when I find myself at a crossroads, and I always choose the best way. God always helps men of conscience who are not attempting to deceive. This time, too, I said to myself, let's go ahead and knock on her door. If she opens up, it will be a good sign. You tell me whether or not this is so."

She replied in a soft voice, "I don't know you yet."

"There is little to know. I am what you see. When you take a coin in your hand, you know its value, and if you take a healthy and ripe fruit in your hand, you know what kind of fruit it is, what it tastes like, and whether it can do you good or harm. This is the same for a faithful man. I am forty-nine years old, and if I have not yet thought of marriage, it is because I have not met a woman I liked. My life is full, though lonely, but I've been used to solitude for a long time. I am a medical doctor and study, work, and research are my life's companions. I am now telling you that I was looking at your land to build a clinic on it, which may not strike you as very cheerful, but which is more useful than anything else. I know that you, too, are lonely, that you love solitude and the simple life. That is why I dared to introduce myself to you. Finally, I must tell you that, apart from my profession, I have some means of my own, which enable me to live independently."

He adjusted himself better in the chair, and slightly more relaxed, resumed with greater confidence: "I am not asking for an immediate answer. Think it over first. Indeed, I want you to think it over. Get some information about me, and above all, give me your friendship. Your house is beautiful," he added, looking around, as the other man had done, "beautiful and clean."

And in a tone of friendship that seemed to dispel the woman's silent concern, he finally said, "So, your niece is married?"

She was glad to be able to speak, avoiding the initial topic of conversation.

"Yes. She made a good marriage to a rich young nobleman, who married her out of pure love."

"Where are they now?"

"They're on their honeymoon. They'll be back soon."

"To live with you?"

"Oh, no!" And since this exclamation struck her as too vigorous, she immediately added, "They neither wish to do so, nor do I expect them to. It is not right to come between two people who love each other, especially in the early days of their union. Love is a great and sacred thing that one must approach as one approaches God, in silence and in adoration.

He briefly sneered. "That is love as you dream of it at the age of fifteen! In reality, it's something else. It's almost always based on material foundations, which soon collapse. And if esteem, friendship, the intent to live a pure and righteous life, consisting more of duties than of pleasures, do not accompany it, the ruin is complete. Nevertheless," he dared to say, after thinking a moment, "I am glad you have such a religious idea of love. That means you have had no disappointments."

"Thank God not," she answered, almost harshly. "I had no reason to give myself illusions and, therefore, to become disillusioned.

The man leaned forward again, then regained his composure so that she would not think he intended to offend her by his innocent insinuation. "Because you are a wise woman…"

"What do you know?" she interrupted at once. "You don't know me. When you get to know me well, perhaps you will change your opinion."

"The important thing is that you allow me to get to know you. This hope alone makes me happy. Many women, precisely the most level-headed, like to make themselves believe the contrary, and they believe it because, in their minds, they would like to be more perfect. Superficial and oblivious women do not know they are so, and above all don't admit to it. What counts in life are works."

"Who knows? Our actions don't always match the way we feel. Life is, after all, a comedy."

"It's what you read about in novels. Real life is something else, at least for me. Don't pretend. Don't lie. Who forces us to appear to be what we're not? At the most, I'll allow lies in order to avoid making a loved one suffer. One can then pretend to be well even if one is ill and hide passion or pain. These are examples, but I repeat, easier to find in books than in reality. It is difficult to pretend. It's not part of human nature."

"But why, then, are newspapers are full of dramas, almost always provoked by deception and betrayal?"

"This shows us precisely that life is not a comedy but a tragedy. And people love to kill and kill themselves rather than endure their own and others' deception."

She was about to reply, to say that there are special cases, people who do not live like most, but what was the use of talking? What did she care, after all, for that man who sat before her like the patient fisherman who, after a long wait, reels in his empty line? No, he couldn't catch any of the serious, murky creatures resembling sea monsters swimming in the dark depths of the soul. Yet she liked his way of speaking, which matched to the elementary truths handed down from parents to children by life itself.

"If everyone thought as you do, life would certainly be easier. But it isn't, unfortunately," she said after a moment's silence.

"And lest you think me an old romantic, I'll tell you about an extraordinary, seemingly fictional case. I know a woman who took another's name in order to understand that other woman's fate, and she succeeded."

The man seemed moved, if not convinced, and strained rather eagerly to hear the details, but she understood the danger and repented. She spoke confusedly about a poor man who had taken the name of a rich friend of his in order to make a woman fall in love and marry him.

"The man's despicable, if he's not an idiot. The woman will never forgive him for deceiving her."

"I don't think so," she said coldly. "After all, she married him even though she knew about the deception."

"There must be hidden reasons, bonds that were meant to unite these two despite their will. In any case, I believe they will never be completely happy. Woe to the man, or to the woman, who lets herself, especially in love, be caught in the net of another's deceit. Everything will go down with her: her fortune, her freedom, even her conscience."

"Even her conscience," she repeated dreamily. "Perhaps it's true. And men know that. I see they know it."

Then he smiled, a smile that transformed his face and gave him an expression of childish mischief. At last, he was beginning to fish something out. "I hope you're not alluding to me as well, Signorina," he said, rising as if to leave. But he did not go. And she had the impression that he had risen in order to dominate her better, or at least to view her from above and examine how he might pin her down and take her. And the way he spoke his words *as well* made her fearful.

The man leaned against the back of the chair as if to hide his small stature and allow only his head to be seen. Indeed, it was a fine, powerful head with thick, wavy hair that gave off a silver sheen that seemed to come from a distant light. On his forehead, above his partly childish and partly feline eyes, the clarity of a horizon could be seen, one that comforts the traveler even if, as he is walking, night suddenly falls. "Listen," he said in a deep, warm voice, "I have already said that I am not rich, but I can also assure you that it's not your wealth that attracts me. I want to tell you everything. After all, I am more romantic than you, despite the fact that, or perhaps because, my profession, confronts me daily with the most sinister and repugnant of life's events. But in the same way that we need to go to the theatre in the evening or read a book of poetry to escape into a world more beautiful than our own, we also create dreams and hopes for ourselves, even without trying. One day this past spring, I was passing by here to look at the land that they had suggested as a possible site constructing a clinic. Looking up, I saw you on the terrace. You struck me as lonely and sad, as if forcibly shut up in this house and exiled from the world. Your eyes met mine, stared at me, and asked me for help. This is the illusion, and almost the obsession, that has possessed me since that day. Wherever I went, your eyes followed me with that look of supplication and passion. And I've come a long way in my imagination to reach you. Now I'm here, and I don't know which of us needs help the most — perhaps both of us need it equally. We're like the pillars of a bridge that's still unfinished. Perhaps it will be enough to hold out our hands to complete the construction."

She bowed her head and at last felt the blood, melted from its chill, flowing in her veins. Here was a man, the one who stood before her, who had truly come to her aid the way someone comes to the aid of another in danger. She instinctively stretched out her hand like a drowning person to a rescuer.

Like the other man, this one took her hand and kissed it with a very different kiss, chaste and tenacious, and it troubled her more. It was a kiss for her alone, the first she had ever received like that.

Then the man sat down next to her on the small sofa and did not let go of her hand, caressing it instead between his own hands, which were soft and fine with extraordinarily velvety skin. They were spiritual hands that seemed to caress only by instinct but were, therefore, more tenacious and sensuous.

He was better off on the sofa than in the armchair. He was able to relax comfortably in the corner, his feet now resting firmly on the carpet. He sat very close to the woman who, after the impulse to let herself go, moved away and pulled herself together, now prickly as a hedgehog but unable to move her hip from contact with his or move her hand from the soft, warm bite of his.

He had taken her and had no intention of leaving her. His eyes, slightly lit up, completed the act of possession, scrutinizing her with a gaze that she escaped but felt flowing over her like warm water. And she felt that the man liked her for that reluctance itself, for that wild scent of chastity, which excited the male and satisfied the suitor.

He said in a voice choked up with emotion, "I thank this hand that I hope never to let go of for the rest of my life. Thank you, my dear, thank you, but don't leave me like that. You look like you're afraid."

"Oh, no," she protested immediately. "Why should I be afraid?"

"I don't know. It seems so to me. Not fear of me, but of men in general. A little while ago you said something that touched me. You said you hadn't suffered disappointments because you never harbored illusions. Explain the true meaning of these words. I think I know everything about you just because I am next to you, and I breathe your breath, but there is something that you're hiding from me. It's the great sadness in your eyes that I would like to know in-depth and be able to dispel. Help me to help you."

Then her fingers lightly responded to his grasp, and their blood rose together like wave meeting wave. "No one has ever spoken to me like that," she said softly, speaking almost in spite of herself. "And never have I believed in anyone as I now believe in you. That is my sorrow, but why didn't we meet before? When we were younger?" she quickly added, as if to offer herself an explanation.

The man then drew his face closer to her face and revealed a secret to her, a secret which they both knew but did not wish to communicate to others. "Aren't we young? Don't you feel that we are?"

At the revelation of this mystery, her eyes glazed with tears. She was alive, then, alive and young, and it was enough to lift her face to drink at last from the cup of pleasure, and all the goods of the earth surrounded her.

"Are you crying?" he asked with the almost fearful astonishment of a child who sees something beautiful but mysterious. "Why are you crying? No, don't do that, it makes me suffer."

She cried loudly, without sobbing, without hiding, almost with joy, like the tree that shakes off the rain that has refreshed it when the wind blows. Indeed, at the light caress of his hand, which brushed her hair and descended to the nape of her neck, unintentionally pressing the clasp of the necklace, she had the impression that the necklace was coming apart and the pearls were running over her body, illuminating it.

"Enough, now. Be calm," he insisted in a voice accented with suffering.

"Let me cry. It does me good. I've never cried before," she said quietly. Now she was the one squeezing his hand for fear he might escape her.

"At last, I really believe I am young," she said, wiping her face and shaking back her head to drive away the shadow of time. "As long as you don't deceive me, too. My life has always been like a foggy morning when one waits for the sun in order to see clearly. Meanwhile, everything is gray, uncertain, dreary. Sometimes outlandish forms appear. They look like people but are bushes or stones. I was twenty years old, and nobody had yet spoken to me of love, because I was not pretty and especially because I was poor. I retreated, humiliated as though I really wasn't worthy of love, though I thought of nothing but love.

"I felt that an injustice was being done to me, and I asked God why he creates us with such a desire for life and then deprives us of it in its essential form. And I was also intelligent, despite not having studied and despite living among poor and ignorant people. Our little village was divided into two infinitely different classes of inhabitants: shepherds and bricklayers. Both of them emigrated, taking turns: the shepherds in winter, the bricklayers in the spring and summer. The former went down with their flocks to warmer areas, the others left in March when the days were longer. They mostly came to work in the city. My desire went with both groups. I was seized by the need to go, though I didn't know where. I just wanted to go. In the meantime, I had to take the sheep to graze, sad and resigned like them.

"My father was a bricklayer, the master builder, in fact, and he too went away every spring. My mother, who was always suffering from arthritis, looked after the house, and I looked after the little flock. Papa wrote as soon as he arrived in town, but afterward only sent a few money orders. Not until early winter did we see him reappear as he had left, wearing the same clothes, his bundle tied to an umbrella, and inside the bundle, a knotted handkerchief with his large earnings.

"He never spoke about his business. He told us nothing about his life in the city. It was as if he were sucked up by his work and seemed to be thinking of something serious, far away. With his fingers and a pen, he was always making calculations.

"In the winter, he worked in the village. He built a church and a new parish hall, all according to his own design, and he built a little house for us. But one winter, he didn't come back. He wrote that he had a big job to do, a whole building for piece-rate pay. After that, he didn't write anymore. It was a sad winter for us, buried under the snow. As in other years, we had entrusted the sheep to a relative, a shepherd who had come down to spend the winter on the plain. I stayed home to watch over Mamma.

"Mamma, who every year was as lively as the plants at the return of the warm season when father came home, wasted away even more that winter. The cold, the worry, and the despondency affected her illness. She went to bed and never got up again. I saw her being extinguished, day by day, like a fire without fuel. Both of us were alone in that great silence of snowflakes falling one on top of the other and petrifying like marble. It was like being in a graveyard with no exit.

"I was too accustomed to silence and solitude to abandon myself to despair. I didn't despair, but neither did I hope. This state left a sinister imprint on my soul, as though it were freezing.

"My mother, on the other hand, burned with passion. Jealous, she thought Papa had stayed in town for some woman and that he might never come back, and she cried on his pillow as if he were dead.

"He had left us enough money to live through the winter. When the flock returned, he finally wrote, ordering the sale of the sheep. The proceeds were to sustain us for the rest of the year; he wrote that he had invested all his earnings in a venture he hoped would be profitable.

"It was the death blow for Mamma. He was certainly maintaining a woman, perhaps another family.

"I insisted on not selling the sheep, partly because I loved them, and we lived in misery all year hoping that he would come back. The others came back, but he didn't. They came back saying incredible things about him: that he was earning fabulous money, that he was buying and selling houses on his own account and on behalf of others, that he lived and dressed luxuriously. Then I decided to go and look for him, but at the last minute, Mamma became very ill and prevented me from leaving. She was afraid of dying alone, and the winter closed our door again, blocking it with sepulchral snow.

"And then at Christmas, he came back. He didn't look like himself anymore. He was so well dressed and prosperous and cheerful. He held fortune in his hand.

"He had come to get us and bring us with him to the city to live permanently. He had brought Mamma a fur coat and pearl earrings as though for a bride. And she died the next day. I think she died of joy.

"We buried her in the little graveyard full of snow with her fur coat and earrings. I wanted to stay up there that winter in order not to leave her alone.

"In the spring, I joined my father, and within a few years, we were rich.

"Wealth did not bring us happiness. My father died young, worried about leaving me alone, and his work unfinished. In order to supervise and complete the construction of a rented building that we owned, I had a cousin come from the village. He was also a bricklayer and a widower with a little girl. One day, he fell from the factory. I must add that he drank, and perhaps, the accident wouldn't have happened otherwise. In any case, I looked after him like a sister, until his death, and I took his child in. I had her study, or rather, you could say that we studied together. I set her up well. Now she is happy, and I am alone again, alone but peaceful."

"Peaceful," she repeated, raising her voice. She had told the last part of her tale quietly with the melancholy monotony of fading light.

The man clasped her fingers, which he had almost let go of, but she withdrew her hand and began to speak again. It was like the sudden rising of the wind in a gray stillness and the laying bare and fiery tinting of the horizon that chases the clouds so they can no longer suffocate it.

"I'm calm, at last, but I've had a sad summer, more terrible than that terrible winter up there when all the bonds of humanity seemed to have been loosened around me. I'll tell you everything. There's no reason to pretend, as you say. I've never been happy, because I haven't had faith. My own niece and I have never understood each other. The irony of my mother's and father's fate and the cruel game of fortune, which mocks those who pursue it, have sucked out the best of my blood, so what remains is like rust in my veins. I continued to live in affluence as in misery with an indefinable weight on my heart, regretting the sadness of the past. To suffer, but at least to believe! And my lack of love has spread over everything. That's the trouble. I have even had marriage proposals, a few men tried to approach me. I rejected all of them, certain that they were after my possessions and not my soul.

"Finally," she resumed, lowering her voice again with a gloomy tone of sadness, "a strange experience has convinced me that life is a game. A man came to ask for my hand in marriage. He was here, in this very drawing-room. I feel like I'm seeing him again. He was handsome, young, intelligent. Above all, he had that sense of adventure that we women like. He is the man we dreamed about in our adolescence, whom we will never meet because he only exists in our imaginations. Well, there he is, in front of me, from a faraway country, come on purpose to look for me, Maria Baldi. Except that I'm not Maria Baldi. She's another woman who, knowing about his search, assumed my name in order to seduce him and take him herself. In short, the fact is this: he came one day to meet me, as you have come today. My niece opened the door to him, and when he asked her if she was Maria Baldi, she said she was. She took him, and they are happy."

The man listened now with an animal-like curiosity, like a dog that hears a suspicious noise. A shadow of jealousy darkened his eyes, which became cruel. Instinctively, he moved away from the woman and sat up straight.

"Now I understand the story about the man who took your friend's name," he said, more to himself than to her. All of a sudden, he thought back, putting together their entire conversation. He weighed each word of hers, as though recalling it by heart, ruminating over it, and growling at it with disgust.

"Yes, that's why you're right to say, 'I don't know you yet.' It's so hard to get to know people. And you're right. Now I understand why you are not taking those two back to your home. Love is a great thing when it's not ridiculous, and it's good not to delude oneself, lest one be disillusioned. But my opinion of you has not changed, although I now know you a little. You are an exceptional woman, and you show through your trust, for which I thank you, that you share my principles of sincerity and loyalty."

She, too, had stiffened again. His somewhat disjointed speech aroused in her a feeling of mistrust. But she saw that he was speaking out of jealousy, and she felt flattered, but in a negative way, partly because she thought he had spoken somewhat ironically.

"What do you think of me?" she asked, turning almost threateningly. As the anger disappeared from his face, and only a frightened sadness remained, she too pulled back, serious and tired.

"I did my duty completely. I could have taken that man back. I only had to want it. He sought my wealth, like the others, because he didn't have enough to be as comfortable in life as he needed. But if I wanted to, I could even make him like me. Don't you like me?" she asked brutally.

"I am different," he answered humbly, yet with malignant intent.

And she defended herself. "You're a man. You're the first real man I've met. Don't diminish yourself because you want to diminish me."

"God forbid! But the other man…"

"The other man was a scoundrel, and I think he still is. I think he married my niece partly out of sensual love, but mostly hoping for my wealth. He is a scoundrel, but he, like all weaklings, has the power of instinctive cunning. I believe he married my niece because he's well aware of the charm his presence aroused in me.

"You love him," said the man, lowering his head like a child about to cry.

"What is love? If it's fear, that mysterious fear that sometimes assails us in a lonely place, of being surprised and violated by a stranger, and the vigilance against danger, and the shame of wishing for it to happen, well, I certainly felt all that until a few days ago. No, to be honest, until a few moments ago, when I felt in you the living heart of a man who can save me and accompany me the rest of the way. If you still hold out your hand to me, I am no longer afraid, and all the past is nothing but a horrid night of bad dreams."

The man immediately stretched out his hand, but something dark must have happened inside him because he turned and hid his face in the corner of the sofa so she thought that he was crying.

What followed was an evening of unforgettable light.

The man went away promising to return the next day, and she wandered about her house as though in a new home. Everything had changed. Objects looked at her with joy, with a warm glow that appeared to her to be from her own eyes. The nightmare had at last evaporated, and she felt that she had confessed and taken communion.

She went out on the terrace and partially took out the necklace. It too seemed more beautiful, enlivened by her warmth. But why had the man gone out of his way to avoid looking at that treasure, which she was neither showing off nor hiding?

Perhaps he thought she was so rich, or he himself was so rich, that he attached no importance to a jewel. Or perhaps he did not know its value, or he may even have believed it was fake.

"It's better this way," she thought, tucking the necklace back into her dress, "for, in the end, it's not ours."

After the meal, served by the maid, with a joy as mute as that of the objects around her, she felt the need to move, to go outside. But the terrace was now too confining for her, and she did not want to go far.

She went down to the meadow and walked around her property. She felt as if she were in the open countryside. The moonlight, not yet corrupted by the lights from town, increased this illusion. The smell of the earth and grass assailed her with a shiver of memories. It was again the scent of youth, the longing for love, the deep breath of the roots that preserve life forever.

To go and go. She wandered through all the paths of the meadow as though it were a continent, and her shadow imitated her, like children playing and swallows flying, until she realized that the servant was, now and then, looking out from the lit window, perhaps mocking her a little. So, then she sat down on a stone in the shadow of the house.

And she thought again about all the things her suitor had said before he left, of his insistence on depicting himself like most men, those who live to enjoy life in its divine simplicity. "For three quarters of the year, even more, I like to work and study, do good for myself and for humanity. But then vacation time comes, and I love to travel, get to know places and countries and new people: and if I can't do it traveling the world, I do it within the walls of the city. Even a small room can be a whole world when one loves life, and we must all be like the Arab who kneels down and thanks God because He has allowed him to quench his thirst at the fountain."

The next morning, while she was combing her hair in front of a small mirror attached to the window handle — both habit and mirror left over from her time of poverty — the servant knocked on the door. Without entering, as though intuiting that she was the bearer of bad news, the servant handed her a letter.

A letter that had been brought by hand. The white, square envelope and the address written in small, black letters, which seemed to have been engraved, struck the woman as sinister. She felt as if she were reading her name on a tombstone.

It was the man, her suitor from the day before, writing to her.

"Please forgive me if I do not return, either today or ever again. You have already understood that I belong to the great number of ordinary men who see life as a straight road and avoid dangers. I will never forget you, but after what you have told me, I cannot marry you."

She did not read the letter again. She tore up the paper and the envelope and threw them out of the window. She then resumed combing her hair, raising the silver locks of her thick hair to her forehead.

She was calm. She found only that the little mirror had suddenly become misty and distorted her pale face veiled by a blue shadow making her nostrils somewhat colorless and swollen, like those of the dying.

She went back to her grooming. She had begun it with some care, brushing her hair first and thinking how she could hide the white hair under the black. Then she went back to styling it as usual, pushing it up and back with indifference and weariness. And she remembered something far away, a day when a tornado had struck her in the middle of her sheep on the little plateau in the village. The sheep had clustered around her, not to seek protection, it seemed, but to protect her. The wind filled her clothes, passed over her neck like a knife, and penetrating from one ear to the other, filled her head with its roar, carrying away her thoughts. And in the distance, the lake fought with the wind, lighting up and darkening under the passing clouds like a night sky streaked with lightning.

When she had twisted and secured her hair, she put her arms by her side and stood as still as she had done at that time, waiting for the whirlwind to stop and her thoughts to return.

They returned. She remembered everything from the day before, and she broke out laughing as if she were life itself, mocking the talk, promises, and hopes of men.

In the mirror, she saw her face lit up by that silent laugh, and she remembered her niece's words: "If he had seen you like this, laughing this way, he would have loved you."

She clenched her teeth in brutal rage. She watched her face become gloomy and light up again like the lake under the whirlwind. Then she took the small mirror that had reflected her face when she was a girl and slammed it against the windowsill. The shards splashed down where she had been sitting the night before, tinkling and glancing off each other with the clatter of coins on stone.

And with that, she felt that she had broken and scattered her past for good.

In November, someone told her that the newlyweds were back. Waiting for the apartment they rented to be ready, they were living in a luxury hotel. She hadn't sent or received any more news from them, but one evening the young bride came alone. She was pregnant. Her face expressed disgust and pain, and she looked so humiliated that her aunt's cold and concealed scorn fell away.

"Forgive me," she said, kissing her timidly while, without speaking, she looked around furtively to greet the familiar objects without seeming to do so. "I have been ill ever since we came here, and I have not telephoned or written so as not to bother you. Also, my husband is offended because you stopped writing. You didn't answer one of his letters, or my last postcards: nothing, nothing."

She spoke in a monotonous voice without rancor or sadness but with the dull tone of someone resigned to everything. And the other woman looked at her with perverse joy. That beautiful and elegant bride, prematurely wearing a golden fur coat, was not happy.

"I waited day after day for the two of you to return," she said quietly. "Each of your letters suggested that you would. I haven't been well myself. I haven't been out. I haven't seen anyone. What was there to write?"

"You could have invited us to stay for a few days," resumed her niece without paying attention to the weight of her words. "The hotel is expensive and uncomfortable. Over the past few days, Giovanni has been going out of his mind about furnishing the house. I think he's gone to all the furniture stores and all the antique dealers. Today, he bought ten embroidered and painted cushions, and brought them all to my room. I felt as if I were suffocating. He also bought valuable paintings."

"It's pleasant to have a nice house, and he likes such things."

"I would, too, if they didn't cost so much and take up so much room. Now, I'll have to work twice as hard to take care of them."

"You'll have a maid look after them."

"I'll be the maid," she said with a slight sneer. "I want to work as I've always worked. Didn't I work here? Weren't you happy with me? Weren't you happy?"

"I was happy, yes. What's wrong, child? You look like you're not happy."

"I'm even too happy. Why shouldn't I be? Because I deceived you two? But believe me, aunt, it's better this way. He wasn't the man for you."

"Maria! Why are you saying such things? Still?"

The young woman then threw down her cloak, which opened up like fresh skin, still violet and copper-plated inside, leaving her clothed in the nudity of a slight, very low-cut, sleeveless pink dress.

"Aunt, do you remember our talk when I told you that I wanted to live truthfully? Well, I have kept my word. I live and want to live truthfully. I may be mad and extravagant, as he tells me, a little jokingly and very seriously, but it is necessary. I can no longer pretend. Whatever happens, happens, but I want to walk a straight and clear path."

The aunt bowed her head slightly. She remembered the words of the man who had passed her by, touching her with the flower of hope. But what was she to say now to this other deluded woman, who without knowing it was also acting out a play of sincerity? There was nothing to do but to smile again, with mockery and bitterness, yet she didn't. "Is your husband a good man?" she asked in a muffled voice.

"He is the best man in the world. And I, I repeat, am happy. Yet I suffer. I'm afraid that the creature inside me must diminish this happiness of mine, which I don't deserve."

"Please stop," said the aunt, half upset and half ironic. "It's clear you don't have any real worries if you play around with such nonsense."

"My husband is good and generous, generous to a fault. If he could, he would bring home all the beggars he meets. In the villa by the sea, there was a young bride who had given birth. Well, he wept thinking of what I will suffer. And everything for him holds something wonderful and deeply meaningful. However, whereas he sees an ideal ending to everything, he is a very sensual man. He likes beautiful women, eating well, and luxurious things. He bought two greyhounds and completely forgot about me when he was with them. Fortunately, he soon tires of the things he owns and disposes of them, certainly without making any profit.

"I hope he won't do that to you," said her aunt, smiling.

"There's nothing to smile about, aunt. Anything can happen. But I am not very afraid of that, at least as long as you still want it to last."

"What do I have to do with anything? Let's not start that again."

"You know that, aunt. He's counting on you to help him when we are completely broke, which will certainly be in a few years. He's been eating away at his fortune since he was born. He eats it naturally, the way the caterpillar eats the leaf on which it was born. Now there are two of us, and soon there will be three of us. And he knows this and doesn't worry about it, partly because he has the illusion of being able to work and earn money. But he's as good at being a lawyer as I am. He's good at being cheated by everyone, and it's useless to delude oneself. He came knocking at this door as though it were the door of fate. For he needs to live, and someone has to help him. He is still like the child of a rich family who thinks only of spending his father's and mother's money while waiting for a lucrative position."

"You frighten me, Maria."

"You shouldn't be frightened or worried about anything. He's incapable of hurting a fly. Where there is no evil, fear should not exist. If you close your door on us, it's possible he'll leave the city and never see you again. His pride is boundless. I came here to see you secretly this evening, because your silence after his letter offends and humiliates him. He will never come to you again unless you not only invite him but also tell him that you deeply love and esteem him. And he deserves to be loved and esteemed, after all," she resumed, surprised by her aunt's harsh silence. "He is good, after all. He is a big child who needs to be guided and held with a firm hand. Unfortunately, I'm not able to do this. I'm not able," she added despondently, letting her arms fall with a gesture of powerlessness. "It is perhaps about class. I feel somewhat like a servant in front of him. I may think badly of him and get angry and foresee the worst things, but in his presence, I make myself feel small. I'm weak, weaker than he is, because, in the end, I love him. Do you understand, aunt? I love him. I love him because he is who he is. If he weren't this way, maybe I wouldn't love him. And then he married me," she resumed, getting up again. As though protesting against herself and all she was saying, she added, "And he didn't have to do it. It's true that he might have done it out of self-interest, but he also did it out of passion. And so far, he has never even hinted at knowing my deception. He is a gentleman with me, even in our deepest intimacy. How can I not be grateful to him? After all, if he spends, he spends his money. I'm ashamed to reproach him. If you knew him well," she said, at last, with an impetus that made her blush, "you would love him, too. You don't know him. You haven't wanted to get to know him. You were only anxious to send us away because, quite rightly, our presence and our love annoyed you."

"You say so many unjust things!" protested the aunt vehemently.

"No, no, you don't love us, and that's bad. One must love, aunt, not in the flesh but in the spirit. Nothing else brings warmth to our lives. What is a person without love? A deceptively luminous bubble. Why haven't you written more often?" she then asked, strangely lowering her voice as though to invite the other woman to confide, to tell the truth.

And the impulse to tell the truth grew in the aunt's veins as well, but she restrained herself. She would have fainted before opening her heart again to a living soul. "I already told you," she answered in a deadened voice. "I didn't know what to write to you. What can a person say who lives as I do?"

"It's not true. You have something against us, something that we must have done to you without meaning to. And you don't forgive; you won't even forgive our child, which is sad, for you as well, sad for your future."

"What do you care about my future? It will be what it will be. And what I wanted it to be. Let go! You have become even more bizarre, and you too would do well to be calmer and to enjoy your happiness more, for your child's sake as well. Besides, your husband's letter was odd. Excuse me for saying so. You're still very young and need to be judicious. Life is a serious thing."

"You don't understand me, aunt, because you don't want to. It's precisely because life is a serious thing that I'm speaking to you the way I am."

"Let it go," repeated the aunt wearily. "Tell me more about your trip and the beautiful things you have seen."

"The trip? Who remembers? It seems to me as if I had already seen all those things in the movies. I would have preferred to stay here. Even at the seaside everything was busy with people, music, excursions here and there. With the vacationers gone, I would have gladly stayed there, partly to save money, but he was getting thinner and paler with boredom. Though he says he's a loner, he can only live among people. He pokes a little fun at everyone and judges his neighbors fiercely, but he can't help it. Now," she went on, noticing her aunt's interest in this chiaroscuro portrait that she was drawing of her husband, "who knows what he's doing with the apartment here. The trouble is, we have two houses, but…" She paused, wrinkling her thin eyebrows, which became bristly. Worry hardened her face, as though from the physical effort of fending off someone who wanted to hurt her.

"But?" asked her aunt, bending and leaning forward with an instinctive benevolence stronger than her hard will.

"I don't mind having that other house, which is in the end our real home. It's sad, you know, but beautiful. And I'm hoping to have my baby there. You won't come? No, you're not coming. I already know that," she said without waiting for an answer. "Yet it will be the moment to forget everything.

"I'm afraid of dying," she resumed, resigned and almost content to speak to herself alone. "Like an instrument that plays music without accompaniment, everything is exhausted, both question and answer. They say that all women have this fear during their first pregnancy, but I believe that, for others, it's only a physical fear, whereas I feel it in the depths of my soul. And if I die, and the baby remains alive, perhaps that would be better. Then, you would love the baby. Everything in life is possible. You're laughing?" she insisted, looking at her aunt with hostility and jealousy. "You're beautiful and young when you laugh. It's a pity that you're always frowning. There, there you go again! Why? Have I offended you? You may marry him. You laugh?"

And the aunt timidly stretched out her silvery, blue-veined arm, as if attempting to caress her niece, who was still leaning toward her. But she didn't move. Only her eyes seemed to reply to the advancing diaphanous hand, which bent and remained suspended, the tips of her nails glistening like frozen tears. Then the same hand reached down to the floor and drew up the cloak but immediately let it fall back down again. For a little while, the conversation seemed to change its tone, for the other hand had risen and rung the bell, and the servant, who appeared so rapidly that she might have been standing just behind the door, was ordered to bring the tea.

"Don't trouble yourself, aunt," begged the young woman. "I had my coffee before I came here. I'd rather smoke a cigarette, if I may."

"Do you smoke?" asked her aunt, surprised.

"Yes, I've got that habit, too. It's nice. I like it. I roll my own cigarettes," she said as though in apology. In the meantime, she had taken the cigarette case and the gold lighter out of her bag. A moment later, the air smelled of an indefinable scent of incense and strong tobacco, which rekindled in the aunt the physical memory of the man who, on a warm, bright evening the previous spring, brought the breath of passion into the house. The young woman, too, had suddenly become excited and beautiful. She stood up and reached for the ashtray on the table, and her pink dress seemed to illuminate the twilight in the room.

"Bring it here," said the aunt.

"No, no, leave it be. It's fine as it is." And placing the ashtray on the edge of the table, she smoked in silence. Every now and then, her bare arm stretched out, and her shining fingernail flicked the ashes from her cigarette. The aunt didn't know why but, each time, this act gave her anguish.

And when she saw that the first cigarette was followed by a second, she rang the bell again and had the tea brought in. When the servant left again, the young woman threw away her cigarette and seemed to shake herself out of a dream.

"You should come, then," she resumed, animated, and it seemed to the aunt, cruelly. "I'm telling you that anything is possible, and you mustn't be afraid to meet your destiny. I want you to answer me."

The aunt answered, but with the resigned tone of someone trying to be patient. "You're fantasizing. Besides, yes, I'll come, if my presence is necessary, but do me a favor and stop with everything else."

"*If your presence is necessary!* For me, your presence is always necessary. If I miss you, if we miss you, maybe the light will go out."

Then the woman had a rush of giddy disdain. "You've come to hurt me," she said despairingly. "No more, I beg you. Don't talk like that anymore. Or, if you're convinced that's the way it is, if you think you are like the fish in the net still in the water, then try to free yourself. But I want to be free, too. And I want to do something painful now that, perhaps, will benefit us all. Both you and I must, from now on, behave like strangers." She waited for the young woman to jump up or cry, but she did not even raise her head. Her niece only reached out again and picked up her fur coat, pulled it tightly around her, and clutched it to her chest as if she suddenly felt cold. She too seemed to take refuge in the things around her.

Then she went away, alone through the rainy evening, among the shadows that crossed the black pavement shimmering with the sinister glow of winter nights. She seemed, in her rich clothing, happiness lost in a place of pain.

The winter that followed was extraordinarily cold and clear. Locked up in her quiet house, the woman felt as though she were in a convent in the mountains. She no longer expected anything. She no longer hoped for anything. She felt as if life had left her in peace because she was content with what she had, with the warmth of the house, the good food, the sun on the terrace, the breath of the meadow white with hoarfrost, which reminded her of her pastures and her supremely sad childhood. It reminded her of the blue of the mountains edged with snow and of the moonlight on windy nights when the closed window shone and creaked as if made of ice.

Snow fell, too, and those were happy days. She felt that she was still up there, a child, amazed at the mystery that transformed the earth and gave things the supernatural charm of ghosts. She remembered touching the snow for the first time after living in fear. It had felt like fire to her. Then she ate it and had never found anything better. She never tired of looking from her window at the white meadow where the birds danced like children in the summer until the sunset colored the snow pink.

Suddenly, she thinks she is dreaming: a man passes by, down in the white desert behind the hedge that looks like a flowering hawthorn. It's the man who was briefly her suitor. She wants to laugh, but something like a violent slap prevents her from doing so and makes her sad and thoughtful. It's as though the man has come as far as her door and has not dared to ring. She also wants to open the windows and call to him, but she cannot. He goes away, and she comes to her senses. What is the use of dreaming? He is the man, she is the woman, eternally separated. They seek each other and do not find each other in the luminous and infinite desert of illusion, and if they manage to meet, they wound each other like enemies.

At Easter, a letter came from her niece, whose mode of expression always seemed strange but matched the truth.

"I'm fine, aunt, and things seem to be going well. However, I continuously feel something like a threat against me, and the remorse over what I have done never leaves me.

"I often feel that I have done you more harm than I believe. Something must have happened to you since Giovanni's last letter to you. I don't know what, but something sad, and a high wall has come between us, and we don't see each other; perhaps we shall never see each other again.

"Giovanni and I never talk about you, but I feel that he thinks as I do. Only at Christmas, he told me that I should wish you Merry Christmas, and I *couldn't*. I believed you would find it hypocritical, so I preferred silence. However, I cannot keep silent any longer. Winter is over, everything in nature is renewed. Why can't this happen for people as well? Therefore, I send you my good wishes, which are also for myself because I hope that, from your peace and your joy, I will receive my heart's greatest desire: your forgiveness."

This letter seemed sincere to the aunt, but it didn't melt her chill. Yet, day by day, she felt the weight of loneliness growing. The hope of finding something to help her live had, after all, always accompanied her. Her alert senses, all the more alive when restrained, had filled the desolate reality of sterile days with desires and illusions. Time had slipped through her fingers like water through an hourglass, inadvertently, but always throbbing and alive.

Now this hope and these desires were missing. Her liveliest senses were slowly dying, leaving space for the more material ones: gluttony, laziness, and the need to sleep. This lack of spirit, which allowed her body to grow fat and heavy, had already given her the sense of death. But her resulting sadness was still a sign of life. You had to shake yourself, reawaken your soul, reconnect with living things, even if it meant pain.

One evening, after Easter, she again put on the necklace, which grew pale as well when not used, and she suddenly thought about the baby that was about to be born, which could have been hers, and in some way was. Without her, it would not be born, and she felt a dark sense of remorse for already burdening the fate of the innocent through the mother's worries and scruples.

Then drowsiness came over her. What's the use of struggling in vain? Alone and overturned as we are in the human chain, life passes us by, and everything dies with us.

The more she became still and alone in the wasteland of her bed, the more she felt that she was walking, walking inexorably. Her heartbeat marked the step, the one that can only be heard in silence, the true step that leads to the great goal.

And then, out of this despair buried by sleep, mysterious dreams sprang up.

Invariably, they involved her dead mother, and while the background resembled a chiaroscuro painting where the landscape, the characters, and the animals moved in a haze of confusion, the figure of her mother occupied the foreground, clear and prominent, always in bed, sick with waiting and useless passion. What was she waiting for? Sometimes in the dream, even her father's figure appeared. She didn't move. She waited all the same.

The woman dreaming identified with her mother, with the pain and the waiting that she had once inhaled and that had remained in her blood like a hereditary disease.

Then, one morning in May, after a night cluttered by these dreams, she received a notice: someone wanted to speak to her on the central telephone. She didn't seem disturbed the way she had been on the morning when she had received the letter from her ludicrous suitor. Yet she felt that something new, perhaps the mysterious event she had unwittingly, almost unknowingly, expected, had come to shake her existence.

Who wished to speak to her from afar? She thought of the man in the baggy suit, but she sensed that it wasn't him. She thought of Maria, but she sensed that it wasn't her niece either. Until the last moment, she was undecided about going, as if it were a dangerous appointment. Then, she went and looked carefully into the telephone booth before entering, almost afraid of a trap.

And in the silence, in the darkness, as in the mystery of an underground cave where a treasure or a monster could be hidden, she heard, distinct but somewhat cavernous, as though from the depths of an excavation, the voice of Giovanni Delys.

And it seemed to her that his voice itself was enclosed by a dark and cold inner void and by the effort to overcome the distance in order to make itself understood by its sound alone rather than by the words being spoken, yet unaware of all this.

He spoke happily, indeed oblivious of past events, so oblivious that he spoke to her informally.

"How are you? How are you?" he insisted.

"Fine," she answered with an indifference that could not have better confirmed her good health.

"Look, excuse me for disturbing you, but it was necessary. It is about Maria. She gave birth this evening to a beautiful girl, and you must come see her. You must," he repeated after a moment of silence during which the whole world seemed dark and uninhabited. "For Maria, you understand. We are in the villa by the sea. If you don't want to travel alone, I'll come and get you. It's necessary. For Maria," he repeated a third time, slowly. Then his voice died away like one who is dying while uttering his last wish.

The woman trembled all over, holding the phone like a lifeline, as though she were hanging from the edge of a precipice. She couldn't respond, and the voice was silent, and she remembered Maria's words: "He is the proudest man in the world." She felt that he would never speak again, like a dead man, if she didn't answer immediately and affirmatively.

"I'll come," she said softly, letting go of the phone as though allowing herself to slide down into the void of the abyss.

Then she went back to listening. The man's voice came now, echoing with relief.

"Thank you. Thank you, you know, for Maria and for the baby, and for me as well," he added, warmly.

She remembered him in the act of kissing her hand with his soft, eager lips, and she saw him all over again, in the flesh there beside her, in the darkness, in the silence, as if he were holding her so as never to leave her again.

He insisted on coming to fetch her, and since she refused, he gave her precise directions for the trip, but without any solicitude. Now that he had secured her promise and was sure it would be kept, his calm voice was that of a happy man. Yet she felt that a mystery lay hidden, an ambush in which she was already caught.

"I'll keep vigil and save myself again. I must be either predestined, or God must have completely abandoned me since I can still be deceived. In any case, Thy will be done, O Lord," she thought, hanging up the phone.

And instinctively she made the sign of the cross.

She left that same night although they were expecting her the evening of the next day. And in the train, alone, worrying about her abandoned house and about the danger she was consciously running into, among the shadows and the unknown figures that came and went, and the mysterious distances crossed, she felt as if she was dreaming her usual dreams.

But the dawning day dispelled the nightmare. As soon as she arrived, the whole fishing village seemed to welcome her with celebrations.

The cottages, situated on the right of the grassy road that flanked the harbor's canal, sheltered under a green and glittering cloud of locust trees, threw down their brick staircases from their high doorways, inviting her to enter. The cats that guarded the thresholds watched her with the impassivity of sacred animals. On the other side of the street, between the trunks of the great gnarled locust trees, along the bank of the canal, hung drapes of old reddish nets and newly woven sandy-colored nets, all of them undulating with their cork ornaments like women's dresses. Through the veil of these nets blazed the crocus of unmoving sails whose reflection kindled and filled the rippling water of the canal with luminous snakes.

An old woman, up early, sitting under a locust tree, spun hemp for the nets. Pulling the thread from a spindle above her, she looked like the site's Fate, the symbol of that simple life whose breath blew with the breath of the earth and the sea.

Other scenes enlivened the grandiose blue background: a boat leaning over the water looked like a wooden house with trees uprooted by the wind with all its primitive furnishings. The green flasks and the baskets smelling of fish spilled out on the quay among the monstrous masses of ropes and planks of the shipyard. Children ran about straddling dogs, and a whole crowd of domestic animals moved aside to make way for a slow procession of waddling white geese.

And on top of a mountain of planks, a barefoot little girl dressed in red, her blond curls penetrated with blue, was crying for fear of not being able to come down again. Below, children mocked her and encouraged her. Everything weeping and laughing added cheerfulness and color to the place.

Further down, the appearance of the village changed. With wells in their clean courtyards like cups on a tray, new houses, belonging to rich fishermen, are reflected in the canal and proud to be in the company of the church and the grand gray villa, solid as a castle, closest to the sea, and completely surrounded by it.

The woman paused, still uncertain and curious. From the tower of the church came the sound of bells, shrill as the cock's crowing that opens the dawn. The canal water, reflecting the church and boats and trees and sky, more beautiful than reality, like in an artist's creation, repeated the sound from an infinite depth.

Before entering the villa, the woman felt she needed to get to know it from the outside, to study its appearance, as if it were a new acquaintance. So, she went ahead, beyond the facade, beyond the wall of a small sandy garden that stretched out beside her. She turned around, but the villa was still above her, heavy and high as a tower.

Then she thought of going as far as the wharf, where she would be able to see it in its entirety. Moving along the wide, undulating beach covered with flowering bushes, she suddenly saw something resembling a small black mountain with peaks of equal height surrounded by snow, motionless against the turquoise sea. It was a row of nuns sitting close together on a sand dune. They were praying, slowly sliding the beads of the rosary as if to count time in that vast solitude. It seemed that, after crossing the world, they had stopped there, at the edge of the earth, to contemplate eternity. A sense of solemn peace emanated from them as though from a mountain landscape.

The woman went further to the strip of stone overlooking the sea. That morning, the sea, blue and calm, allowed itself to be dominated. When she was seated at the top of the quay, she had the impression that the water was flowing out of the earth like a river without boundaries going calmly towards the horizon. The air, the space, the intensity of all that blue gave her a sense of inebriation. She was afraid of falling into the water and looked towards the ground to find a place to rest.

The villa was there in front of her. She could see three sides of it, the central one jutting out towards the sea like the prow of a ship, with the crenelated tower above which two white pigeons radiant as alabaster circled. A loggia of marble and another one of iron, smaller but higher, surrounded that whole side of the villa. And on the highest balustrade she saw something even more cheerful and candid than the pigeons in love: the new-born baby's diapers hanging out to dry.

But she immediately turned against her turbulent feelings. She didn't want to become more emotional. The same intoxication that the morning and that grandeur of solitude gave her made her freedom seem more precious. And she wanted to save her freedom, like life itself, at any cost.

And she sat down, bent over, opened the purse in her lap, took out the necklace, and spread it on her knees to warm it in the sun.

The pearls, which had become slightly yellowed again, suddenly brightened. The blue reflection of the air gave them an iridescent violet light, and it was as though the blood of their mysterious life was reawakened.

She had brought the necklace to give it to the baby girl as an offering to life itself, but she wished that they would finally leave her in peace, just as one leaves the dead.

The closed door of the villa, sheltered on three stone steps and protected by the loggia on the upper floor, reminded her of the one at her own home. Recently painted, it too reflected the surrounding green and blue, and in the brass studs she saw her face so grotesquely deformed, wide and cackling, that she almost felt cheerful.

But she, too, like that man once at her door, could not ring immediately. She felt that this little door, refurbished to deceive the visitor's eyes and hide the decrepitude and decay of the villa, mocked her with its sneering studs as well as with the height of the doorbell, which she would have to lift her whole arm to press, perhaps not even reaching it.

It struck her that only people of very high stature were allowed to enter the villa. Indeed, everything in the rigid facade peeling from the gnawing sea wind was high: the floors, the windows, the loggias, the cornices. This grandeur, poor and powerless like that of old fallen lords, could interest but not intimidate.

And the woman felt as though she were standing before a painting, and she had been given a varnish to remove its essential poverty and dull color. Her heart and instinct did not deceive her. Behind that embellished door there was misery in need of help and pain hiding almost fearfully like a sick animal.

But the same contrast between the darkness taking refuge behind those closed windows, faded and furrowed with cracks, and the bright light from outside, kept her frozen on those steps as though on the top of a mountain when evening is falling and the danger of solitude destroys the beauty of the place and time.

Descend and leave! There was still time. She went down a step, then up again, stood on her tiptoes, and rang the bell.

After a long wait, an old woman, looking like the wax portrait of a queen in exile, dressed all in black with a lace cap in the fashion of fifty years earlier, opened the door for her. And the open door let out a stench of damp mixed with the smell of incense as though from an underground church.

The old woman must have already been warned. She seemed to recognize the visitor and invited her to enter the grand, dusty, stone-paved hallway lit by a large window high above the steep staircase of corroded bricks.

"How is the Signora?"

"She's well," said the old woman in a barely audible voice as she went up the stairs, keeping close to the wall, behind the other woman. And she seemed unwilling to say anything more.

The footsteps, though light, resounded in the great clear silence of the stairwell, which revealed a certain dignity in its poor, worn, and lifeless steps. From the window, the staircase resembled one in a lighthouse, so much so that the sea below and the sky above were of the same intense, almost palpable, blue. On the first landing was a long corridor, all windows and doors, and that scent of incense, which penetrated the air, came from there. The old woman, going straight up the second flight, explained the mystery: "The nuns are in there."

The second landing was the same as the first, only the corridor was narrower, with small round, slit-like windows, and a broken floor that looked as if it had been trampled by soldiers. To excuse the bad state of affairs, the woman explained, "There were refugees."

From the back came a beam of light, as if from a terrace on the sea. And from that bright glow, the man who had called her sprang with a silent swiftness, which revealed his eager anxiety.

As on the first day that they had met, he was dressed in black with the same expression on his face, between old and very young, the same straight posture. His eyes were calm with a deliberate calmness that couldn't hide a depth of sadness. Even now, he made a move to kiss her hand, but only from an instinct, which he immediately conquered. The two hands brushed against each other and escaped like two enemies who meet out of necessity and avoid each other.

"How's Maria?"

"Fine, thank you. We were expecting you this evening, but I think she already knows you've arrived. We'll see her now. You have no baggage?" he asked, looking back as he led her down the corridor.

"No. I can't stay long," she said softly.

"Never mind. Thank you for coming."

He spoke softly, too. He bowed his head as if to remember something, then turned to the old woman who was following behind them close to the wall.

"Is the Signora's room ready?

"It's ready. This is it," said the old woman touching a doorway.

He pushed the door, and through the wide-open window across the room, which let onto the iron loggia, shone the turquoise arch of the sea.

"You will need to wash and have something to eat and drink," he said, pushing the woman lightly by the shoulders. "Please excuse me if you do not find the comforts of home here."

"It doesn't matter," she said almost roughly, without entering the room. "I would like to see Maria at once."

"Right away. Let me tell her. In the meantime, have something. Come in."

She obeyed, again overcome by an anguished sense of mystery. The old woman, after saying to her, "Here's water. I will bring you some coffee," left her alone in that large, tall, bare room furnished only with a small bed and a serpentine chest of drawers with a cracked mirror. In spite of the great light and the warm air that came in through the open window on the loggia, she shivered with the cold, and with fear, as if they had locked her there by force and were condemning her to remain forever in that desolate solitude.

But suddenly, even before the old woman reappeared, a strange sound called her attention. In the great silence, it seemed to be there, in the room itself, at short intervals, like the faint sound of a violin. Then it seemed to her like the moaning of a small animal she couldn't identify. At last, she recognized the wailing of a new-born child.

It must be the baby girl in the adjoining room trying out her new voice that penetrated through the crack in the doorway like a new string, squeaking a little, but already with a strong sound and a tone of wailing and singing. The woman thought they had put the baby there on purpose so that the two of them could meet without any other introduction or witnesses: the two of them alone, listening to each other in the light and the silence. In spite of her diffidence, she approached the door with an impulse of tenderness and curiosity and also of gratitude for the voice that broke that sinister spell.

She tried to open the door. It was locked, and the key in the keyhole didn't allow her to see through. She then remembered observing from the pier that all the windows in the corner of the villa looked out at the iron loggia, and she went out onto that loggia, making it easy for her to enter the room next door.

It was a room exactly like hers, painted in lime with turquoise squiggles on the ceiling that looked like a play on the reflections of the sea and with the same serpentine chest of drawers and the grotesque mirror with the clusters in the frame resembling raisins and earth-colored apples. On the same little bed, between two pillows that served as a cradle, lay the baby covered by a green veil.

She approached on tiptoe and looked down upon her, fearful of disturbing her even by breathing, and stared at her as though she were a strange thing never before seen. She was bound tightly up to the neck like a dangerous being that had to be prevented from fighting. Under the veil, the round, peach-colored face would have given her the impression of a fruit veiled by green leaves were it not for the mouth that twisted into continuous grimaces of disgust and the milk-painted eyes, open and staring.

Slowly, as if pushed there against her will, she bent down, not so much to see the baby as to understand her better, without the emotion that she should have felt and on which the others counted, but also without hostility. In fact, she felt a kind of cordial benevolence, as if the baby girl could understand and become her friend.

The child was no longer moving, in fact, but continued her grimaces, which seemed to express her inner thoughts: the exhausting questions of why she was there, why she was already hungry and already in pain, and already feeling abandoned, and the mystery of that great shadow that was bending over her little by little, to offer help that did not come from the heart.

When the woman had almost reached the edge of the veil, the baby's little face shriveled all over, and a sharp, animalistic screeching came from her mouth like so many arrows. The woman rose up in fear, repulsed and hurt.

No one came. Why did no one come?

The baby fell silent, and all was quiet again in this place that indeed gave the impression of being in a dream.

But wasn't it really a dream? The woman remembered her other dreams, which were clearer in their outward appearance than the actual events yet cloaked by the twilight of the mystery within. To shake herself awake, she went out again onto the loggia, looked into her room, and saw on the little table the tray with the coffee and breakfast that had been brought by the old woman. The old woman had disappeared again, and as though it were poisoned, she was afraid to drink the coffee. She was afraid of everything and had to free herself. She took the necklace and went into the adjoining room, knelt down in front of the little bed, lifted the veil, lifted the little baby's warm head, as though fearful of crushing it, and she fastened the string of pearls on her neck. Then she readjusted the veil and felt as if she had thrown the necklace into the depths of the sea.

And as though he had been spying from the shadows, waiting for that moment, the man immediately reappeared, and so quickly and silently that she had no time to get up. But she was not ashamed to be caught in that act of offering, and at least everything was over as quickly as possible.

"Well," he asked softly, leaning over her, "do you like her?"

"She's beautiful," the woman said softly, trying to rise. The man then took her hand and put it on the baby's head, pressing a little and lightly stroking her hair with the tips of her fingers, to make kneeling before the child less onerous.

"She's beautiful, yes," he repeated in a low, calm voice that held the sinister breath of evil revelations. "And we hope she'll be happy. And she'll bring happiness to you too, because you will love her. Why did you put that necklace on her? Do you intend to die?"

"I'm already dead," she said, hiding her face in her hands. And she shuddered all over, for she felt that this was the revelation. And she longed to let herself fall, defeated by his hand, and actually die.

"We shall never die," he resumed, "so long as a spark of love, even if it has the appearance of hate, germinates in us like seed in the frozen earth. And it is not in our power to extinguish this spark, even with the death of the body, for it is our part in God."

"Words...words,..." she murmured.

Then he withdrew his hand and resumed in a harsh voice, "Pick up the child. Look at her. You have given her a burden that you think you can get rid of, but which will oppress you more than ever. She was already united to you, even without this chain, as we are all united, dead and living, in error and atonement. Pick her up. You haven't looked at her yet."

"Giovanni!" she groaned, taking his hand and kissing it. Why did she kiss his hand? Why was she trembling all over, as if he were speaking to her of love, and rather than offering her the child, he was offering himself?

But he pulled back his hand and clenched it in a fist that shook with protest, repentance, and impotence. At last, she felt all the deceit of her vain fears. Yet the anguish did not leave her, and the man's words pressed against her more than his hand on her head. She tried again to free herself. She rose and brushed off her clothes as though after a fall. She looked at him with hostility, as though to challenge him.

Then he bent down, and it seemed his panting breath moved the veil. He picked up the baby and placed her into the woman's hands, forcing her to turn into the full light. And with a feeling of vertigo, she realized that the child's eyes would not close, stillborn in the vain light of earth.

This Book Was Completed on 27 January 2023
At Italica Press in Bristol UK.
It Was Typeset in Adobe
Garamond Pro &
Wingdings.

Made in the USA
Las Vegas, NV
16 September 2023

77660888R00073